'MAROON BOY

When Matthew Morten went to sea in 1568, he was a Bible-reading merchant's apprentice and the youngest hand aboard the *The Golden Way*. He returned four years later with a reputation that included mutiny, raiding, and the nickname "'Maroon Boy".

'Maroon is short for Cimaroon, a name given to escaped slaves who fought the Spanish in Panama and the English in Jamaica. It is known that Drake joined forces with the Cimaroons at one time, to harass the Spaniards: but where he was seeking gold, the Cimaroons wanted revenge on the white man.

Matthew Morten's motivations were even more complicated – though he didn't realise consciously what they were. Why he did what he did adds a fascinating moral dimension to this tale of swash-buckling adventure.

Robert Leeson

'MAROON BOY

Fontana Lions

First published in Great Britain 1974
by William Collins Sons & Co. Ltd
First published in Fontana Lions 1982
8 Grafton Street, London W1X 3LA
Second impression December 1985

Fontana Lions is an imprint of
Fontana Paperbacks, a division
of the Collins Publishing Group

Printed in Great Britain by
William Collins Sons & Co. Ltd, Glasgow

For Christine and Fred

'Maroon is short for Cimaroon, a name given to escaped slaves who fought the Spanish in Panama and the English in Jamaica. They were skilled guerrilla fighters and their resistance lasted two centuries.

Some parts of this story are from real life. John Hawkins and Drake did make the voyages mentioned; Hawkins did bombard Baron Wacheren's ships when they sailed up Plymouth Sound and the Flemish prisoners did escape, though how, no one truly knows.

Drake did join with the Cimaroons near Nombre de Dios to harass the Spaniards. He admired their courage and way of life.

Matthew Morten's story, like that of Susannah, John Galton the helmsman, Abraham Combe the merchant, Sir Henry Ferrers and his arrogant son Charles, is not "real" – but it could have been.

If you go to Plymouth you will find The Hoe, Notte Street, Vauxhall Street, Breton-side, Stillman Street still there, though much changed from those times when Elizabeth was on the throne and Matthew raced Charles Ferrers round the walls.

Plymouth is proud of its Elizabethan past, but time and Hitler's bombs have destroyed many of its traces. The Plymouth of this story I have recreated from old records, maps and walks round the streets of the modern city.

But I must acknowledge the help of the Librarian and Staff of Plymouth Libraries and the inspiration of Crispin Gill's "Plymouth: A New History".

R. L.

Chapter one

"Matthew!"

The wind barely stirred the short grass where Matthew lay, book clutched in his hand. His eyes were fixed on the waters of Plymouth Sound some half a mile away beyond the walls of the town.

"Matthew!"

The voice called again, closer, but still below him and out of sight. Now the caller seemed anxious. But Matthew did not move. His eyes were on the water where the setting sun caught the mast of a full-laden cog crossing the gap between the Hoe and Mount Edgcombe. On board some brightly polished metal flashed in the light. Matthew screwed up his eyes, lowered his head, pressed his face into the turf.

"Matthew, lad. Can't you hear your mother calling? Haste, lad, thy father's home. They've crossed the Crabtree ford already. Shame on ye if you aren't there to greet him."

Now it was Old Tom, their neighbour, calling. Matthew could hear the old man and his mother as they struggled up the last few yards. They were so close he could hear their breathing. But he lay still and waited. He wanted to hear his mother call again, for her voice always pleased him.

She would sing as she spun wool and he played in the cottage. She had taught him the old songs and they would sing together. And the songs would stop only when his father tramped into the kitchen, great shoulders turned sideways to clear the doorway.

When the Queen's men had come to take his father away, Matthew had gone to earn his threepence a day, herding sheep on the slopes beyond the town walls. But his mother and he still played the game they had always played. When evening came and time for supper, his mother would call his name and he would hide. He would crouch down wherever he was and would not answer. She would call him three times and he would not stir. Then she would sing:

"Hot pies, pies all hot,
Hot pies for your supper."

She baked the best pies in Plymouth and sold them to the merchants' houses – the Hawkinses in Kinterbury Street, the Combes in Stillman Street. Her voice was known everywhere. And on Sunday in church when psalms were sung, people would fall silent and hear Mistress Morten as she sang the verse. But at sunset, the song was just for Matthew.

Now, though, his mother's voice was not teasing, but strained and anxious. And Matthew did not hide himself for play. He hid because he wished that what was going to happen would not happen. For five years, while his father lay in jail, life had been hard for both of them. They had lived on the little his mother could earn from baking and spinning and the few pence Matthew got for herding sheep. But still these had been happy years. His work had not been too hard. As he watched the flock he would read the books given him by the chantry priest, an old man who had stayed in the town when the monks and friars left and the merchants bought up the friary buildings. Matthew knew his Bible – his father had seen to that in many a hard lesson by candlelight on dark winter evenings. But from the old priest he had learned Latin, and discovered books of strange tales written by travellers to far countries – Africa to the south, the Americas to the west.

Matthew lifted his head from the grass. The cog had

sailed out of sight. The sun's golden gleam was fading in the sky to the west.

An idea which had lurked at the back of his mind ever since he had been told his father was coming home, now forced itself forward. He clenched his fists tight, pressed them into the ground and suddenly sprang up, just as his mother and Old Tom reached the brow of the hill. His mother was as small and straight as Old Tom was tall and bent. Her cheeks were rosy as a girl's, her eyes clear blue, though her hair was white. She was cross with Matthew, he could see. But still she smiled a little.

"Here I am, Mother, I was reading."

Old Tom grumbled.

"You'd read your head off, young Matthew." The old man bent awkwardly and picked up the small leather-bound book.

"What's this? I can't make out a word on it. This is not good English, that's for sure," he said.

"No, 'tis Latin."

"What do you want with Latin? Only pope's men read that."

"Come, Matthew," said his mother quietly. Matthew followed her slowly down the hill, while Tom came after, turning the book's pages.

"Jacob Morten's son, reading Latin . . ."

He caught up with Matthew and his mother, who had linked arms and were half running, half sliding down the grassy slope.

"Did not thy father say, Matthew," he panted. "The word of the Lord in the tongue of his own people is all a man wants or needs."

Mistress Morten turned at the foot of the slope.

"There's no lad in Plymouth better schooled in the Bible in his own tongue than Matthew. But scholars know more than the Bible. When the new school is opened he shall go there – now that his father has.come home."

"Our Matthew a scholar. That's rare, now. But what's in this book, Matthew?" The old man held out the small volume and Matthew took it.

" 'Tis by an Italian merchant who has sailed to the Americas. He tells of strange lands, strange folk, strange beasts."

"Hm. I can hear strange tales like that in the Golden Fleece down by Sutton Pool, from Hawkins's and Lovell's men. But I don't have to believe 'em, so why should a scholar?"

As they talked, the three had left the grassy slope and joined the Tavistock Road. They quickened their pace, for the Old Town Gate would shut at eight.

Tom repeated his question: "Eh, Matthew. Why should thou credit these stories?"

"I might take ship and sail to the West myself and find out."

The words burst from Matthew. His mother stopped in the dusty road, her cheeks suddenly pale.

"Matthew, that's no matter for a jest."

Matthew's fists clenched.

"I am not jesting, Mother. Lads no older than I have sailed to Newfoundland with the fishing boats."

"That's no way to talk, lad, with thy father coming home after five long years," said Tom.

Matthew did not answer. They trudged in silence through the Old Town Gate and on to the waste land where the cottages and gardens lay. But the thought came again into Matthew's mind.

"Now my father's come home, I can go away."

Old Tom left them at the cottage door.

"I'll walk to the Market Cross and see if I can catch a sight of them."

The cottage, whose whitewashed walls caught the last faint glow from the sun, was simple but roomy. On one side a high kitchen with a tiny dairy at the back. On the other a shippen that could hold the Mortens' few cattle in winter. Above that a bedroom divided by a heavy curtain, where Matthew and his mother slept. On the kitchen table supper was spread, with wooden platters, earthenware bowls and pewter tankards, lent by a neighbour for the occasion. At the side of the fireplace steam rose from pots and pie-dishes. Matthew's mouth watered and he forgot his troubled thoughts. Turning, he squeezed his mother. She reached up slightly for now he was taller than her, and ruffled his hair. They started to sing:

"Hot pies, pies all hot."

Then they laughed and walked to the door to wait for Matthew's father. Outside the light was fading. The town buildings faded. But Matthew's keen eye caught a group of men coming from the street behind St Andrew's Church.

"Will that be Father?" he asked.

His mother nodded. But suddenly she looked anxious and turned her head away. Was she crying? Matthew tried to ask her why, but the words did not come. Now his eyes had found something strange about the group of men who came nearer to the cottage. There were five, it seemed. One, hurrying in front, was Old Tom. The other four walked close together, as though they were soldiers marching in step.

Or as though they were carrying something.

Alarmed, Matthew turned. The tears were running openly down his mother's cheeks.

"Mother, what is it?"

The men, with Old Tom stumbling before them, stopped in front of the cottage. Mistress Morten ran to them. And now Matthew saw that they carried between them a stretcher. Matthew stared. On the stretcher lay a long, gaunt man, his hair quite white. This was Jacob Morten, his father, that black-haired, furious giant of a man whom the Queen's officers had dragged away five years before, clutching his brass-bound Bible.

Old Tom pulled at Matthew's jacket.

"Aye, Matthew. Thus they serve the Lord's servants. I fear, lad, thy father will never walk again."

Matthew's breath stopped in his throat. It seemed his chest would burst. Pity for his father struggled with all the fear he felt at the sight of the remembered face. And behind this fear and pity was a strange angry voice, deep within him, saying:

"Now I can never take ship and sail away."

Chapter two

Now that his father was home again, Matthew was told that he must stay at home – no more herding sheep. In his feeble husky voice, Jacob Morten said: "I need Matthew by me now. My eyes do not see so well. He must read for me." And read Matthew did, by the hour, in the evenings when the cottage was quiet, and the visitors who streamed there each day had gone home.

And there was more than reading. His father, once so powerful, now had to be washed and dressed every day, and this Matthew and his mother must do. He marvelled to see how his father's ribs stood out through their thin clothing of flesh – "Like the prison bars," said Jacob grimly – and the painfully thin legs, their sinews twisted and helpless. A ship's barber came up from the port to cut the thick, matted hair and trim the tangled beard. He taught Matthew how to wield the razor, and from that day on this was the boy's task.

It was impossible to carry Jacob up the narrow steps to the bedroom over the shippen. So a bed was made up for him on his stretcher in the kitchen. A lean spinster from Market Street came one day carrying a pillow for Jacob's head. "The best for thee, Jacob Morten," she said. "No straw in a sack."

"Thank ye," he replied solemnly. "Though I have lain my head on a wood-log for five years now."

Not everyone who came brought gifts. Some came to

stare, to pry, to talk by the hour, to eat Mistress Morten's pies and drink her ale. But whoever came, Jacob received them like a king, offering hospitality in a lordly style. When his wife looked worried, he raised his gnarled hand:

"Peace, wife. The Lord has provided and will do so again."

The fear Matthew had once felt for his father now began to fade. It is hard to fear someone whom you dress and wash like a baby. But there was still a distance between them. Matthew read for his father from the Bible and the books of Tyndale and Calvin out of duty, not pleasure. Beyond that, Matthew felt as though his father were someone he had never known, whose past was a mystery.

One day, a huge man in green doublet and vast white collar, over which a dozen flabby chins seemed to pour, came to the cottage with three other men. Some of them were among those who had borne Jacob Morten home.

Jacob's thin cheeks flushed. He called out weakly, "Abraham Combe. Welcome. Come in. Matthew, the stools. Wife, bring ale."

Combe sat down, his bulk spreading so far beyond the stool that Matthew wondered if it would carry his weight. The fat man whom he knew as one of Plymouth's richest merchants, with a tall house, shop and warehouse by Sutton Pool, greeted Matthew's mother with genial courtesy. But he declined all refreshment to the disappointment of his companions.

He gripped Matthew's shoulder and grunted: "Well, they tell me Matthew Morten's a chip off the old block. They say he can recite the Bible backwards."

"Nay, that were sin to do that," replied Matthew hastily, and Combe's friends chuckled. "There, Abraham. Th'art truly answered. Out of the mouths of babes and sucklings..." said one. Combe smiled so broadly his eyes seemed to vanish in the creases of his pale face.

"I'll not have thee sin, Matthew, not Jacob's son. May

you grow up like him. Our land needs many Jacob Mortens. Who was it dared bring the true Bible from Geneva when Queen Mary forbade honest men to read the Lord's word in their own tongue?"

"Bloody Mary, mindst thou," muttered one of Combe's friends, then added when he saw Mistress Morten frown. "Begging your pardon, but that word shall stay with her name for ever. The blood of good men is on her head. And there Jacob lies, thanks to her. Is it not so, Jacob?"

"Aye," said Jacob. "Three years as guest to Queen Mary – and then two years as guest of Queen Elizabeth. Forget not. The true faith is still not secure."

"No," added Combe, "not while the Queen seeks friends in France and Spain."

The others nodded. Then one grinned. "They did tell us in Exeter that Queen Bess would not free Jacob Morten, for he was a mortal dangerous man."

"Aye," said another, "mortal dangerous to the Queen's officers." A gust of laughter rose from the table. The speaker turned to Matthew.

"Thou'd be too young to know. But we saw thy father fell four soldiers and chase the rest all down New Street."

Mistress Morten raised her fingers to her lips, but the speaker, excited, ignored her and went on:

"And when the Cornish rebels broke down our walls and set the Guildhall afire, who was it held the Old Town Gate to the last, thrust for thrust. Not for nothing did men call Jacob Morten . . ."

"Peace." The word came like a gasp from Jacob's lips. But it silenced the room. "The past is past. A man learns the error of his ways and turns to goodness. Enough," he commanded.

A moment's embarrassed silence followed. Combe dragged his bulk from the stool. "Come, brothers. Let's away. Let Jacob rest and Mistress Morten get back to her baking. Her pies are worth more than all your prating."

But he stopped at the door. "I'll wager Hawkins has not been near thee, Jacob."

Jacob's head wagged slowly. Combe's face purpled. "Ah, 'tis fine to parade to church with your crews, and say prayers twice a day on ship board. But all for show. Now that fine Mr Hawkins runs the town with his friends, marries the Navy Treasurer's daughter, and has the court gallants buying shares in his vessels, he's no time for a man who has done more for the faith than ten John Hawkinses."

"Peace, Abraham," said one of his friends. "Thou'lt burst for rage." Laughing, they trooped across the cottage yard. But Combe, whose face now took on its normal pale colour, stopped and whispered to Mistress Morten, "Aught that you lack, do but speak and Abraham Combe will provide."

But Combe was wrong about his rival. A day had barely passed when a knock brought Matthew to the door. Outside in the yard stood two seamen with great bundles on their shoulders. Behind them stood an elegant man with neat pointed beard resting on a sparkling white ruffed collar. Matthew's mother called out in surprise.

"Why, Jacob, 'tis Mr John Hawkins."

"Bring him in with all speed, then," croaked Jacob. But Hawkins was already in the doorway, directing his men to unpack their bundles and spread out white linen sheets and thick quilts.

"Welcome home to Plymouth, though I be late with the welcome, Jacob Morten. I came from London only yesterday and bring something to help thee lie more softly."

Jacob nodded his thanks and bade Hawkins sit down. But he waved his hand and remained standing near the door, while his men finished unpacking their bundles and left.

"I hear you plan another voyage, Mr Hawkins," said Mistress Morten.

"Aye," returned Hawkins. "All's ready. We shall sail, with three ships and two hundred men, next week. We shall sail the three-legged way."

"Sir, what can that mean, three-legged?" Matthew burst in eagerly.

Hawkins laughed. "Sailor's talk, lad. Down with the south-easterlies to the King of Portugal's realms in Africa. That's one leg. Over the ocean to the west by the trade winds to the coast of Terra Firma, the mainland of New Spain, to the pearl fisheries of Margarita, to Rio Hacha and Nombre de Dios, where the Spanish King's writ runs. That's the second leg. Then, with good fortune, catch the westerlies through the Florida passage and away home. Buy on the first leg, sell on the second, and pray for rain on the third."

"Why so, sir? And why, with good fortune . . ."

"Hush, Matthew," said his mother. But Hawkins laughed.

"Why, Matthew, then. If we have bad fortune and are caught by the easterlies in the great gulf, we shall be cast on the rocks of New Spain and be food for the fishes. And if it rain not when we sail for home, with empty barrels, we shall perish for thirst and all the gold in New Spain will not bring us into Plymouth Sound alive."

Hawkins looked carefully at Matthew.

"Thou do have more of thy mother in thee than thy father. Thou will not grow tall, but be strong for all that. Is it your fancy to sail? I have places for boys aboard *The Swallow*."

Jacob coughed. Hawkins paused. "Ah, I forgot. Your father will need thee here at home. And I have need of thy father, which is my chief errand now I have brought him my greetings."

"What does John Hawkins want with Jacob Morten, then?" said Jacob huskily. There was a wheedling note in his father's voice that made Matthew feel uneasy.

"Next Sunday my crews go to service before we set sail. It is our wish, every man and boy of us, that Jacob Morten shall read the lesson and say a prayer for our good fortune and safe homecoming."

He smiled as he saw Jacob nod. "Good. On Sunday, then,

four of my best men from *The Swallow* will come to bear you to church."

With that John Hawkins bade the Mortens good day and left. Jacob's face flushed dark with pride and pleasure. Again Matthew had the faint feeling of puzzlement and discomfort inside him. Questions rose in his mind, and later that day, when the tallow dips were lit, he started to ask his mother.

But Jacob called hoarsely. "Matthew, get the Book and read to me."

Chapter three

On Sunday, Jacob Morten was carried to church by four seamen from Hawkins's ship, *The Swallow*. Jacob, his beard newly trimmed by Matthew that morning, his head and shoulders propped up by pillows, thin hands clutching the great, brass-bound Bible, lay on his stretcher, his wife and son walking on either side. As the party crossed the fields, neighbours left their cottages and walked discreetly behind in their Sunday best.

At the church two hundred Hawkins's men were drawn up in ranks in new shirts, linen breeches and woollen stockings. To the side stood the soberly dressed Plymouth merchants and their families. Beyond them, among the gravestones, were the journeymen and apprentices and the poorer people. As Jacob and his family passed through the church door, the seamen followed and then the people flocked in. Jacob's stretcher, a little raised up, was placed near the pulpit, and from his station at his father's side, Matthew could study the congregation – the massed white and brown of the sailors, the dark browns, greens and blacks of the council members, and here and there a splash of red and blue in the fine dress of a gentleman's family.

The church now overflowed and the great doors were bolted back so that a crowd of poorer people who could not get in stood in the porch and churchyard to hear the service. Matthew could see women weeping quietly, wives of seamen who would not see their husbands again for a year or more.

Some might never see them again. Hawkins was careful with his crews but even he could not protect all from sickness or shipwreck. The seamen were straight-faced, but their eyes were fixed on Jacob and the Bible open at his chest. His father would pray for their safe return, and Matthew suddenly realised that for some that prayer would be answered. For some it would have no avail.

Jacob looked down at his Bible, slowly fingered the pages and moved his lips. Matthew had a strange feeling inside him – like cold fire, that froze and burned at the same time. So tense and painful was this feeling he barely noticed that the service had begun.

To ease himself, he let his eyes wander again over the congregation. On the farther side his eye caught a tall, elegantly dressed man, scarlet cloth gleaming through the slashes of his doublet, a foam of lace at his throat. The colours mocked the quieter hues of merchants and their wives, just as the arrogant face with its curled moustache and pale, piercing blue eyes seemed to challenge the whole congregation. This was Sir Henry Ferrers, younger son of a famous family. He had little land but was a famous soldier of fortune. He had fought on land and sea for nearly forty years, sometimes for King Henry, then for Queen Mary, now for Queen Bess. And when they had no need of a sword, or troop of men, Sir Henry served the princes of France, Spain or Italy.

At his side was a boy, likewise richly dressed, equally handsome and arrogant. His eyes, too, roved the church, and now the boys' glances met for a moment, before young Ferrers's eyes with a quick flash of amused contempt moved on. Against his will, Matthew followed the line of the boy's gaze to the centre of the church. There sat Abraham Combe, vast chins solemnly resting on vast white collar. Next, as lean and sharp as Abraham was gross, Mistress Combe. And to her right – Matthew stared. There sat a girl with chestnut-coloured hair, bright cheeks and wide brown eyes, so beautiful the boy's eyes widened. This must be Combe's daughter, though Matthew could not remember seeing her before.

The congregation was silent, waiting for his father. Matthew saw the sinews of Jacob's hand twist as he gripped the Bible — so tightly the leather binding seemed to crumple. But he did not read. The silence deepened. The people waited. Matthew saw the stringy muscles of his father's neck contort, the bones in his face work up and down. The lips moved. But no sound came out. His father could not speak. Something had happened, in the terrible excitement of the moment, to take his voice away.

Again Matthew's stomach was gripped by the freezing-burning sensation. His head swam. He drew in a deep breath and pressed back on the base of the pulpit forcing himself farther up the steps. In the body of the church people stared and whispered to one another. Suddenly there was silence. Then:

"O, give thanks unto the Lord, for he is good . . ."

The voice, clear and well pitched, rang out beneath the vaulted roof. The congregation stared, hundreds of eyes were fixed on Matthew. Yet he could not grasp that it was his voice they heard. It seemed someone else spoke and he, Matthew Morten, listened.

"They that go down to the sea in ships,"

He felt the eyes of the seamen on him.

"They cry to the Lord in their trouble . . ."

His eyes met those of the Combe girl, challenging, yet serious.

"He maketh the storm a calm, so that the waves thereof are still . . ."

Matthew's muscles relaxed. The icy fire died out inside him. He was reciting the lesson as he had done a score of times for his father, so often he no longer needed to read the words. The psalm neared its end. On impulse Matthew turned to the Ferrers family.

"He poureth contempt upon princes and causeth them to

wander in the wilderness . . . yet setteth he the poor on high . . ." His eyes met those of the Ferrers boy again and looked through them.

Then the psalm was at an end. A great whispering sound rose as though everyone let go their breath.

Outside, after service, Jacob Morten's stretcher was set on the grass and the people swarmed to shake his hand. Abraham Combe was there, his ham-like fist grasping first Jacob's then Matthew's hand. "Well done, Matthew. A worthy son of your father." But Matthew saw only the girl with her brown eyes, now smiling mischievously.

The Combes went and in their place stood Sir Henry and his son. "Canst take an example, Charles," said Sir Henry. "If thou learned thy lessons like young Morten, thou and I would be friends."

As the boys' eyes clashed briefly, Sir Henry bent close to Jacob.

"Well, then, old 'Right-hand'. How goes it? Our ways have lain apart these many years. But it grieves me to see you lie there like that."

Jacob's voice strained through his lips.

"You are kind, Sir Henry. The Lord has been good in the end to me and mine."

"And thy son. I see the way you'll have him go."

"Aye, the Lord's way."

Sir Henry smiled grimly, beckoned to his son, and the two turned across the churchyard to where servants held their horses. Now others pressed around with their praises. But Matthew barely heard them.

That evening, when candles were lit, he whispered to his mother: "By what name did Sir Henry call my father?"

But she shook her head. "Ask no questions, Matthew."

Chapter four

Autumn passed into winter. Every Sunday Matthew and his father were called to join in services, sometimes in villages and towns as far away as Tavistock and Exeter. People would crowd round to see Jacob Morten, the "Plymouth martyr". But it was Matthew they came to hear. Try as he might, Jacob could not raise his voice above a husky whisper. Amid the crowds he would smile and nod, his face flushed with pride. At home in the evenings he would fall silent or sit, lips moving, while Matthew read to him.

Matthew never felt again the wild excitement of that day in church. But he would speak the verses with pleasure, feeling the pleasure of people who heard him. Sometimes they went to the private chapels of merchants or gentlemen who wanted a simpler form of worship. And these services he liked best. It seemed people did not simply listen to lesson, prayers or sermon, but silently joined in. The faces of the poorer people at the back would gleam with the contentment of those who dream pleasant dreams. Lines would vanish from their faces, the skin softened as the cares of the everyday world lifted from them for an evening. When Matthew and his mother led the singing, shoulders would sway gently in rhythm with the old tunes, eyes would close as though the world were far away.

One evening, Abraham Combe held such a service in the Broad Chamber of his high house in Stillman Street, near the harbour. The windows jutting over the street caught the setting sun so that the long wall with its panelling gave off a mellow glow. When the service was over, the sun had set and Abraham had candles brought in. He asked the Mortens to stay behind and take refreshment with his family.

Matthew sat by his mother's side in the window seat. He could see in the candlelight the face of Combe's daughter. The half-darkness of the room gave him courage, and when she glanced at him he looked boldly back. His mother nudged him.

"Matthew, Mr Combe is speaking to you."

"No matter," wheezed Combe. "Matthew will learn to give heed when he's in my employ."

Employ? Matthew's hand went to his mouth. What was Abraham Combe talking about? Combe laughed.

"I have asked thy parents, Matthew, if they'll agree to bind you apprentice to me."

Matthew's heart thumped. It seemed the whole room would hear it. But Combe misunderstood his silence.

"You will learn merchandising, service in my shop, help keep my books, oversee my cargoes in Sutton Pool, speak with ships' captains on my behalf. And you shall not leave your studies. I have young people in my household that cannot read nor write. You shall teach them to write their names and read the Word. What do you say?"

Jacob Morten hissed through his teeth.

"Speak up, Matthew."

Mistress Morten came to his rescue. "The lad is struck dumb with surprise, Mr Combe. He'll answer you by and by. Not so, Matthew?"

Matthew blushed and nodded his head. Combe laughed.

"I'll take that for aye. My clerk shall draw up documents and you shall start on Monday morning."

So it was settled. Matthew's life took a new turn and from now on the Combe house was his world. As winter drew on he would hurry home in the afternoon darkness, full of new things to tell his mother.

Abraham Combe was reckoned among the ten richest men in Plymouth, though not as rich as the Hawkins family, who, he often remarked, could buy and sell the whole town. Combe owned no ships but had a half or quarter share in a fair number, ships that sailed to the Newfoundland fisheries or on the coastal trade, or were hired to carry troops in the French wars, now drawing to an end. Other merchants put money into ships that led a double life – now merchant, now privateer. They seized and stripped ships of other nations. But Abraham Combe kept clear of that. At first Matthew thought he looked down on privateering as wicked. But one day he overheard a conversation with other traders over wine, in the counting house above the Broad Chamber. Combe had asked him to bring up the ledgers and Matthew had lingered a moment.

"Aye," said Combe, "there's quick advantage, quick profit in privateering. But a man must think of the future. Today we fight France and our lads may seize French ships. Tomorrow we are at peace and down come the Lord High Admiral's men and you're charged with piracy."

"But Abraham, the Lord Admiral has no authority in Plymouth, now we have our charter."

"Look ye. If it suits the court to sweeten the Kings of France or Spain by jailing some English merchant with no friends in London, I don't give much for our town's freedom. And see," he went on. "Now the French are at war with one another. Protestant fights Catholic. Some think it smart to sail under French orders to plunder Frenchmen. But I say there's no safety in it. No, let our court and Queen Bess say clearly where this nation stands, today and tomorrow, before I'll venture hard-earned wealth in privateering."

"Hawkins and his brother do well enough from it, Abraham."

Abraham pounded the table in sudden rage. "Don't talk

to me of Hawkins." Then suddenly he looked round. "Matthew, don't stand and gape. Take these books below."

Matthew enjoyed his work in the shop. Combe dabbled in all kinds of trade: wine, silk, nails, coal, raisins, pepper, mustard, soap, lengths of cloth and barrels of fish. The shop and store were crammed with casks and bundles. The air was full of the wildest mixture of smells. Soon Matthew learnt the prices, learnt to tell one customer from another. Some might have credit. Some might not, for they were "bad debts" or even "desperate debtors".

But most of all he liked the quiet moments when he taught the young servants, two small boys and a girl. He liked to see their round eyes when they heard the old tales from the Scriptures, or their glee when they read the simplest words for themselves. Their pleasure called to his mind the pleasure in the eyes of the poor people at the back of the rooms at service time.

But there was one pleasure more. Sometimes as they sat in the courtyard he would look up from his reading and see Combe's daughter pause on her way across the gallery to smile quickly down on them.

One day, little Mary, the girl who took her lessons from him, came to the shop and said, "Miss Susannah would speak with thee, Matthew."

Matthew took off his apron, brushed meal-dust from his shirt front, rubbed at a mark on his stocking and then raced up the stairs. The sitting-room lay behind the Broad Chamber and there Matthew knocked and waited. Mistress Combe opened the door.

"Matthew. Miss Susannah is to take a basket to an old woman of our household who dwells now on Breton-side. Mr Combe will not have her go to Breton-side alone. You shall go with her."

Matthew rushed down the stairs and waited impatiently in the street. But it was some time before Susannah came down. Her hair, which had been bound in church, now fell to her shoulders, shining reddish brown against the green of her gown. Matthew brushed again at the meal-dust on his clothes. But Susannah did not seem to notice. She set off rapidly towards the harbour.

"Ought we to go by the quays?" asked Matthew anxiously.

"Why, art afraid?" asked Susannah pertly.

"Your father . . ."

"My father bid thee go with me, not tell me where I should go."

Then she smiled. "Nay, Matthew. 'Twas only in jest. Come, let us be friends."

"Gladly," he replied. Soon they were pushing their way through the crowded jetties alongside Sutton Pool – through the littered cargo, the tangle of netting and cordage, the crowds of shouting, sweating men loading the broad-beamed cogs that rose and fell in the water.

Then the Pool was behind them and they had reached St Martyn's Gate. Beyond lay Breton-side, a dismal sprawl of poor huts and hovels outside the wall. The Breton-side boys would fight the boys from the Old Town, and now Matthew looked rapidly from side to side, in case he should spot any Breton boy out to pay off old scores. Susannah seemed heedless of danger. Her attention was on the edge of her gown, which she lifted clear of the puddles and mud as she leapt nimbly from one rut to another.

The errand done, they turned to enter the Martyn Gate again. But a strange procession blocked their way. Three men and two women with small children, all filthy and ragged, trudged through the gate. As they went they cursed and shouted and Matthew looked at Susannah to see if she understood the meaning of the vagabonds' foul oaths. But she only gazed at them half in wonder, half in pity. Then she gasped as through the gate came the town beadle and constable, bundles of twigs in their hands. Whenever one of the tramps seemed to loiter a blow would fall and the victim would turn and curse more violently. Slowly, noisily, the procession moved off, men and women shouting, children howling.

"Why does he beat them so?" asked Susannah.

Matthew shrugged. "They are not people of this parish. They are beggars and have no licence to stay here. They must move on, back to where they came from. If they will not go, the beadle beats them out."

"But it is cruel."

"If a man will not work, neither shall he eat," replied Matthew. "Let them go back to the place where they were born and find work there."

"You are hard, for all your piety, Matthew Morten. Are they not God's creatures, and shall we not pity them, at least?"

Matthew turned in anger.

"When my father was taken from us and thrown into prison, though he had done no wrong, my mother and I, we did not beg. No, we worked and lived only on what we might earn. Let them do likewise."

He marched off in front, his cheeks still hot with anger. Susannah, shaking her head, followed him at a little distance, and they returned to Stillman Street in silence.

Chapter five

At home, Matthew's father seemed to recover from his gloom after what had happened in church. Under Mistress Morten's care, his health improved. The thin face began to put on flesh. As strength returned, his voice grew stronger, rose above a whisper. But when he tried to read aloud from the Bible, after a few verses he would have a fit of coughing and call hoarsely for something to wet his throat.

Matthew noticed another change. His father's way of dress had become more elegant. Though he lay on his couch, well wrapped in covers to protect him from the cold late autumn air, he would insist on being fully clothed, down to fine black hose and shoes. Every three days there must be a clean white shirt. And these shirts were not plain but edged with lace. Mistress Morten must starch them well, and Jacob would pull at the collar until he was satisfied it sat well. Then he would set his face sternly, fold his arms and settle down to gaze out of the kitchen door to see who might come to visit him.

When he had helped his mother in the early morning to make his father ready for the day, Matthew was glad to run away from the house, across the fields and through the alleys to Stillman Street. He was never late for work. But he always ran as though he wanted to get away from home quickly.

But in the evenings he would find his father dozing after an afternoon with visitors. Then he could talk to his mother and recapture the comfort of earlier years. He would answer her questions about his work. She would quiz him about Mistress Combe's household, or ask him in a gentle teasing way if he had seen Susannah. And he would bend his head over his platter to hide his embarrassment.

In these quiet moments over supper he tried to coax his mother to talk about his father's past life, to throw light on these hints of violence and evil. But his mother would say "the past is past". Yet still he would wonder.

Even more he puzzled over his family's new prosperity. As an apprentice he received no money from Abraham Combe. His mother no longer sold pies. But there was food in the house and his father dressed in style. He hesitated to ask his mother to explain, though, for he sensed that she too was uncomfortable.

Baffled at home, and hurt by the fact that Susannah seemed now to ignore him, Matthew found his chief pleasure in teaching the little servants. Most of all he enjoyed the company of little Mary. She was ten years old, pale and thin, with large, almost black eyes. Her dress, cut down for her from clothes handed down by someone else, fitted her badly. Sometimes she tripped over it as she ran. She ran everywhere and when she sat for her lesson would fidget all the time. But her eyes gleamed with cheerful curiosity. Her questions were endless. And she would often contradict Matthew.

And when she did so, she would begin, "My father saith . . ."

"My father saith, that the whale could not swallow Jonah, for the whale be but a small eater and eats no flesh."

"My father saith, Adam were more to blame than Eve. For if a man say – my wife bid me – others will mock him."

"My father saith . . . 'twas unjust of God to agree with Satan to torment Job."

The boys would nudge each other and giggle, while Matthew looked round nervously to see if anyone else had heard.

He decided that one day he would persuade Mary to take him home to her father so that he might confront him and dispute his ideas of the Scriptures. But Mary's father, a helmsman on one of Hawkins's ships, was now away on voyage.

One morning, as Matthew closed his Bible after a lesson, he heard his name called from the gallery. His heart jumped. Susannah, in cloak and hood, leaned over the gallery rail, speaking softly and glancing quickly behind her.

"Matthew, if you be still not angry with me, will you come with me for an hour?"

"To Breton-side?"

"Nay, to the Hoe. The lads are shooting at target and I would see them, but I may not go alone."

Matthew hastened to get his jacket and ran to the street door. Outside the sky was grey and a sharp wind blew down from the moors to the north-east. Susannah came down the side stairs and they walked through the gate to the Hoe.

Climbing the grassy slopes, they found the wind blew more keenly. Out in the Sound white wave caps raced. The open stretches of the Hoe were deserted, save for a small group of lads at the butts. Matthew's eye caught the flash of red and grey from the doublet of the tallest youth and realised with a sudden sinking feeling that it was Charles Ferrers. As Susannah and Matthew drew near, Ferrers turned and saluted the girl by raising his feathered cap and bowing from the waist. Matthew he met with a level insolent gaze.

"Are we come too late?" gasped Susannah, breathless from her haste and the cold.

"Nay," said Ferrers. "We had done, but for your pleasure we will shoot another match."

He strolled to his companions, spoke briefly with them. Then taking aim, he sent three shafts whistling into the target. Even to Matthew's unpractised eye, the shots were well placed. None of the other lads who followed could out-shoot Ferrers. Susannah, her cheeks bright, clapped her hands. Ferrers walked back towards them, smiling thinly.

"Will our friend" – the word seemed an insult – "draw a bow with us?" he asked, nodding towards Matthew, but speaking to Susannah.

"Nay, Charles," chuckled one of his friends. "Morten has a good eye for a text, but I doubt he can hit a target."

Amid the laughter, Matthew angrily choked back the polite refusal he had intended to make. Silently he took the bow, walked back to the mark, and accepted three arrows from one of Ferrers's friends. The lad whispered to him, "Watch the wind, Morten, it blows from the land."

But in his anger and hurt pride, Matthew barely heeded. The first arrow missed by a yard. White-faced and gritting his teeth, he drew again. This time the arrow grazed the target. The third shot struck the outer ring, but so feebly that the shaft dropped from the target. He walked back to where Charles Ferrers chatted idly to Susannah. Ferrers laughed.

"Art right, Colin. Morten has a better eye for a text."

"I know nought of archery," burst out Matthew. "But perhaps there are skills I have which others have not."

"Well, I'll allow I cannot quote my Bible backwards," replied Ferrers.

"Nay, Charles, that was unfairly spoken. Morten has offered thee no offence." The lad who had warned Matthew about the wind direction now walked up behind them.

"I accept the rebuke," said Ferrers easily. "Let Morten have his chance. Let him name a test at which I may fail and we shall see. Except it be a text from Deuteronomy, for there I allow I'm a dunce."

Now everyone laughed, including Susannah. But Matthew stayed angrily silent. The lad behind him touched him lightly on the elbow. "Name a trial, Morten."

Matthew sucked in a deep breath. The air stung his lungs.

"I'll race you round the Old Town walls, by Sutton Quay, out by Martyn Gate and round the top."

Ferrers began to laugh, but the others cut him short.

"Go to, Charles. Hast breath in thy lungs. Morten has the right to name the test."

Ferrers, feeling Susannah's eye on him, forced a smile.

"Very well. Miss Combe shall let her kerchief fall and the first one to pick it up is the winner. Agreed, Morten?"

Matthew nodded and drew off his jacket, letting it fall on the turf. The wind cut his bare arms, but inside he felt slow heat grow. More than once, on Freedom Day, he had led the Old Town lads in a race round the walls. He knew the distance to a yard, knew where to hold his pace and where to take advantage of slope and smooth going. He stretched his legs, swung his arms and looked at Susannah. Charles drew off his scarlet jacket.

"Ready?"

"Go."

The green kerchief fluttered down and the two were off, Ferrers at a great pace, Matthew more slowly. As Matthew ran in through the Hoe Gate, Ferrers had gone before him and faintly on the wind came the mocking laughter of Charles's friends.

Along Notte Street Matthew kept the white, grey and red of Ferrers's shirt and doublet in sight and held his own pace. Now they neared the Parade by Sutton Harbour and Matthew noticed grimly that Ferrers was running himself out. He slowly lengthened his stride. Soon they were running along Custom Quay and Dung Quay, dodging the sailors loafing in the shelter of the ships. Past the end of Vauxhall Street and now out by St Martyn's Gate and around the edges of Breton-side. The dismal hovels looked even more grim under the lowering grey sky, and as he pounded along Matthew wondered which was little Mary's home. The thought somehow made him put on speed and soon the clip of his feet made Ferrers turn – teeth gleaming, eyes bulging as he fought for air.

But still he could not resist provoking Matthew.

"Hast a text for this, preacher?"

"Aye," shouted Matthew. "Verily the race is not to the swift, nor the battle to the strong."

And with that he drew up to Ferrers, kept pace for a step and then forged ahead up the slope towards the Old Town Gate. As he crossed the Tavistock Road, Ferrers was falling back. Heart beating evenly, a smile on his lips, Matthew ran on. A quick look back as he turned the north-west corner of the walls and headed south. No sign of Ferrers. But Matthew took no risks. He increased his speed and counted rhythmically. Before he had reached four score, the Frankfort Gate was in sight. This was the last gate and once round the corner ahead he would be back on the Hoe. The ground now began to climb steeply and his pace slackened. He glanced round quickly as he neared the corner. He was alone. Had Ferrers given up?

Now, round the corner and climbing the Hoe, a bare hundred yards from the archery butts where Susannah waited. Eyes down, Matthew clenched his fists and put on a final burst of speed.

He opened his eyes to laughter and ironical cheers. Ferrers's friends stood in front of him, and in their midst, holding up Susannah's kerchief, stood Ferrers. His face was pale, his chest heaved, but in his eyes was the glint of victory.

Matthew halted a yard away from him.

"Cheat, Ferrers, cheat," he gasped. "I passed you in Breton-side and never saw you again. You clipped the course. You ran in by the Old Town Gate and out again by the Frankfort Gate. Admit it. You cheated."

Ferrers grinned. "Let Miss Susannah be our judge. Did I or did I not come round on to the Hoe a good four score paces in front of Morten?"

Susannah nodded.

" 'Tis true, Matthew. Thou'rt beaten, I fear."

"Nay. How could you see that Ferrers cut across from gate to gate, for the walls would hide him. I know and so does Ferrers. He has cheated."

Ferrers stepped forward.

"Those words cannot be unsaid, Morten. But thou shall eat them."

One of the lads laid a hand on Ferrers's arm. He shook it off.

"Nay, I'll not draw on a 'prentice lad. But I'll take it from his hide with a quarter staff. Go bring them, Colin."

The lad brought two staves and cast them in the air. Charles caught his easily, Matthew missed, the stick grazing his knuckles.

Charles motioned back the others. Matthew stole a quick glance at Susannah, but the girl's eyes were turned to the ground. An instant later, Charles lunged at him.

It was no fight. The staff in Charles's hand whirled like a windmill and Matthew was hard put to keep its smiting, jabbing, slashing blows from his chest, arms and legs. Down came the staff on his knuckles, right on to the newly opened graze. With a gasp he opened his fingers and dropped his staff. Next the point of Ferrers' stave drove into his belly, forcing the breath from his mouth in a shrieking gasp. As he turned up his face to fight for breath, he barely saw the shadow of the blow that crashed on to his temple, throwing him to the ground. Then all was dark.

He opened his eyes to pain and cold. Someone was pulling at his shoulders, vainly trying to raise him from the ground.

"Matthew, dear Matthew. Do be up. 'Tis snowing. Thou'll catch thy death."

He struggled to sit up. Crouching beside him, her little face blue with cold, her hair frosted with newly fallen snow, was Mary.

"Miss Susannah sent me to bring thee home."

Chapter six

With little Mary anxiously holding his arm, Matthew staggered back to Stillman Street. Mary took him down the side passage to the Combes' kitchen, where the cook found goose grease to rub on his bruises, and a bowl of hot water to wash the blood and dirt from his face. He told the curious servants that he had fallen on the road.

Back in the shop he found Abraham Combe waiting, wagging his huge chin, his eyes grim.

"And where has Master Morten been? Shall I have an apprentice and serve in shop myself?"

Matthew began to explain, but Combe's questions were only for form's sake. It was clear that he knew what had happened. Then to the boy's astonishment, he said:

"Go home now. Tell thy parents I sent thee. Get to bed and come back tomorrow, if thy head pains thee not."

And as Matthew turned gratefully to leave the shop, Combe added a parting shot.

"It is nought to me if a hard-working lad should slip away now and then on his own ventures. But do me this service. Mix not my daughter in thy business. She has another road in life. Now get thee home."

So thick was Matthew's head with his bruising and the cold that he was nearly home before the full injustice of Combe's words struck him. Anger made his hurts burn more and he pressed on home through the thickly falling snow.

His mother turned pale at the sight of his face and quickly urged him upstairs to his bed, bringing extra covers and, best of all, a bowl of broth. Matthew stretched his legs out in the warmth and looked through the tiny window under the eaves to the roof of St Andrew's now covered with snow. Soon he slept. Next day he was in a fever and his beaten head had swollen so that his left eye could not open. His mother gave him a herb drink and he drifted off to sleep again. He woke again when it was night and the town quiet under its blanket of snow. His mother crept to his bedside and gave him more of the herb brew. In the morning he woke briefly. There was a message from Mistress Combe that he should rest and get well. And a small pot of crab apple jelly. In the waxed top, someone had written with a pin, "Matthew Well". The letters were large and written with great effort. It was Mary's first use of the letters he had taught her. He smiled and the action pulled the skin round his wounds and made him cry out.

Next day was Sunday. His mother came to tell him that to everyone's amazement, his father had read the lesson unaided. True, people at the back had been unable to hear, and some had grumbled to themselves that Matthew had not been there.

On the fifth day he was wakened by the sun's rays slanting into the room. The narrow strip of sky seen from his bed was clear and blue, the air cold. But he felt well again. Next day he dressed and went outside, but sank up to his breeches in snow.

Cattle had been driven indoors and he helped his mother feed them with kale, remembering wryly the winter when he and his mother had eaten the kale themselves and the stock had died. Things were better this year, though how he could not rightly say.

Back at the Combes' he was told that Susannah was in Exeter staying with well-to-do cousins. His mother, an Exeter woman herself, said, "In Exeter, wealthy is wealthy."

To which Jacob Morten muttered, "And in Exeter, pride is pride."

Business in the port was at a standstill and Matthew found few reasons to go about the town. But one day by chance he met the lad who had befriended him at the archery butts on the Hoe. He greeted Matthew civilly and told him that Ferrers had been sent away by his father to Oxford. "Though 'tis a waste of the learned doctor's's time. Charles would have chosen to go with his father to Malta where a fleet is gathering to fight the Turk. He'll make a soldier, will Charles, but no scholar."

"Why should Charles Ferrers despise me so?" asked Matthew.

"Despise thee, Morten? Not he. He hates thee."

"Why hate, then?"

"On two scores. His father twits him over thy skill in learning, and . . ."

"And the second score . . . ?" urged Matthew.

The lad smiled. "Bethink you where you work, Morten. Farewell." And with that he was away, leaving Matthew baffled.

That winter Matthew gave his lessons in a corner of the kitchen, for the courtyard, open to the sky, was too cold. The two boy servants had barely learned to write their names and read a few simple verses. But Mary could read and write with ease, and it was in her progress that Matthew's chief pleasure lay. For months now Mary had barely spoken of her father, except to wish he were home and that things were easier for her family. She was the eldest and her mother was sickly. Matthew silently blamed his own stupidity and went to speak with Mistress Combe.

To his surprise, she was cool and uninterested. "Mary we clothe and feed and pay twopence a day. But the Galton family is not at our charge. John Galton is a Hawkins's man."

Pondering this, Matthew spoke with his mother. "Well

now, Matthew. John Galton is helmsman on a Hawkins's vessel. And 'tis true, when seamen are on a long voyage, it goes hard with their families. You know how it was with us when Father was in prison. But if all goes well, John Galton will come home with money in his pocket."

"And if he dies at sea, or be maimed?"

"Then he or his kin will have a licence to beg around the churches."

"A licence to beg? Poor Mary. But Mother. Can we help them?"

"How help them, son?"

"We have money. I have seen Father count it."

His mother smiled thinly. "Aye, and he has plans for every penny piece."

"But Mother."

"See, lad. Do you bid Mary to pass by our door when she goes home. She shall have supper for the little ones."

So it was. But one day, when spring was advanced, Mary came tripping into the shop, her face glowing.

"Up at Kinterbury Street, they do say that the fleet is to come home soon."

"Then thy father will come with a bag of gold."

Mary's face grew serious.

"An' he come home safe and sound is all my wish."

Soon enough the watchman on Rame Head lit his beacon for Hawkins's ships back from the Americas. Rumours flew round the port. The fleet had lost twenty men with fever. A ship had been seized by the Spaniards and Hawkins was sailing to see the King of Spain to claim it back.

"They tell me," grunted Abraham over his wine in the Broad Chamber, "that he calls Philip of Spain 'my good master'."

"What does it count what he calls Philip of Spain, so long as he gets back his cargo?" retorted one of his friends.

"Aye," said another. "They tell me that in one vessel

alone he has brought goods twenty times the value of his cargo. There's advantage for ye."

Abraham snorted. But his friends mocked him.

" 'Tis well for thee, Combe, that never ventured more than a quarter share in a seacoal tub that do sneak round the coast, to call a man who sails the wide sea."

Abraham's cheeks purpled.

"You'll find Hawkins is not the only venturer, even if he hath the favour of the court."

"Eh, Abraham, what signifies that?" demanded his companions.

"Ha," said Abraham, as though he had already spoken too freely. "Those that wait see much."

Hawkins's ships did come back laden with the riches of the Caribbean coasts and islands. He was now without doubt the richest man in Plymouth, if not in Devon. Another such voyage, men said, would make him the richest man in the kingdom.

But they came back with the fever too. Within days of the ships unloading came news that returning seamen had brought the fever to Breton-side. A watch was put on the Martyn Gate to try to stop the sickness spreading to the Old Town.

When Mary did not come to the Combes' shop, Matthew believed at first that she had stayed away to welcome her father home. But she did not come the second day, nor the third. A sudden fear struck Matthew. He left the shop, went through the storeroom and out into the courtyard where one of the servants sat cutting vegetables for a stew. The girl did not raise her head, but muttered that Mistress Combe had told Mary she must stay away from the house until the fever had died down in Breton-side.

"But has no one word whether Mary be sick or no?"

The girl shook her head.

Matthew raced back into the shop, stumbling over bales on the storeroom floor. He snatched up his jacket and rushed out into the street. In his haste he did not look about him, and collided with someone in the doorway.

"Why, Matthew Morten. Why so hasty away?"

Matthew stopped. There stood Susannah whom he had not seen since Christmas. She was taller and, now dressed in blue, her chestnut hair arranged neatly under a bonnet, she seemed even more beautiful. But Matthew only half noticed this. He answered tersely.

"I'm away to Breton-side, to see how Mary fares. No one here knows and neither do they care."

"But the plague is in Breton-side. No one can go there."

" 'Tis not the plague. 'Tis a ship fever. And if Mary's family are sick, we must help them. If they have not sickened, then we must help them come away from Breton-side."

"But Matthew, that is perilous. You will come to harm yourself."

He stiffened.

"And you, Miss Combe, did once talk to me of pity – and in Breton-side, too."

"An' I did, what then?"

"Then you did rebuke me with empty words."

She paled. "Matthew . . ."

He pushed past her. "I have no time for words." He set off down the street.

"Wait, Matthew." She hurried after him, her bonnet hanging on one side. He said nothing, but hastened on. As they passed the end of Vauxhall Street and neared the gate, he paused.

"Nay, the watch is on the Martyn Gate. Let us rather go out by the other side, as though we were set to go to Stone-house. Then we go round about across the Saltash Road and the Tavistock Road and so come into Breton-side from the north. No one will see us, and we may return the same way."

As they walked, Susannah looked now and then at Matthew, but he stubbornly kept his glance straight ahead. But as they reached the Tavistock Road she said: "Matthew, thou art still wroth with me for the hurt you had on the Hoe."

He turned to her. "Not for the hurt. But for a double injustice."

"Double. How so?"

"One that you believed Ferrers and not me when I said he cheated."

She shrugged.

"Second that you told your father it was I who took you to the Hoe."

Her cheeks flamed red. She stopped in front of him and prevented him from going farther.

"That is not so, Matthew. I did say no such thing."

"But thy father . . ."

"My father saith what sorteth with him best. But me he punished. Thee he did not."

"How punished?"

"Do you think that I went of my own free will to my cousins in Exeter?"

Matthew did not answer. His heart was lighter, but he was still bewildered. He hastened his step. Breton-side and its hovels came into sight. A strange pungent smell was in the air. Black smoke rose.

"What is that?"

"They burn wet broom and mull vinegar to clean the houses. Bed straw and clothes are burnt, where people have died," replied Matthew. Susannah paled. She said nothing but matched her pace with his. On either side were tumble-down hovels, doors swinging open or boarded with crossed planks and daubed red. It took them some time to find Mary's home.

A tiny dwelling, it could have no more than one room. But it stood apart, and some attempt had been made to cultivate a small patch with vegetables and flowers. The door stood open, creaking to and fro. But there was no one about. They halted and looked round. Susannah's hand rose to her mouth. Matthew sensed her alarm and felt his own fear stir within him. But he forced himself to step up to the threshold.

"Is anyone there?" he called. Then more loudly. "Mary, 'tis me, Matthew . . . and Susannah Combe."

But the only sound was the creaking of the door.

Matthew drew a deep breath and put one foot into the room. It was in half-darkness. A rustling sound marked where a rat scuttled for a corner. Matthew took one more hesitant step and stopped. Against the wall, where faint light from the door fell, was a rough canvas pallet, straw-filled, half-covered by a ragged blanket.

Mary lay there, head and pitifully thin shoulders uncovered. The face amid the tangled hair was white and still. The black eyes stared upwards towards the roof. Susannah, who had followed him, gave a gasp. They both turned and stumbled from the room into the open air, the clear sky and the smell of the vinegar and smouldering broom.

As they ran through the tiny garden, their eyes bulging with fear, their way was suddenly blocked. In front of them stood a lanky man with arms that swung and brushed his thigh, where a cutlass scabbard hung from a belt. He was dressed in a dirty brown jacket and canvas breeches. His hair, escaping from the thong that held it, fell to his shoulders. His brown, seamed face was divided almost in two by a jagged, grey-pink scar that vanished beneath an eye-patch. His voice was harsh and hostile.

"Have you seen plenty, then? Aye, she's dead, poor little thing, like her brothers and her sisters and her mother."

The man lunged forward and thrust his terrible face into Susannah's.

"And tell me. Tell me. Why am I not dead as well?"

Susannah shrieked, leapt to the side, gripped hold of Matthew's hand, and together they fled, blundering down the road and into the arms of the watch on the Martyn Gate.

Chapter seven

Faced with the stern questions of the captain of the watch, Matthew stayed silent. But Susannah, with a skill that took Matthew's breath away, told a story of walking on the headlands and straying into Breton-side without thinking. They had seen the plague-fires and had run away in fear. So they were let through the gate and, still clutching hands, ran through the back streets to the Combe house. Susannah quickly recovered her calm.

She freed her hand from his and, turning at the foot of the stairs, said smiling:

"See now, Matthew Morten, that my father hears nought of this or I shall swear thou dragged me there against my will." And she pressed his hand swiftly and ran up the stairs.

No more was said of what had happened. The weeks of summer passed slowly. The fever died out in Breton-side, and several score hovels and huts were cleared. A new girl came in Mary's place, but she paid little attention to Matthew's teaching. He would lose interest in the reading and allow his mind to wander. Before him rose a picture of little Mary's face, chalk-white against the straw, then her father's, lean, brown, scarred and angry. Matthew would shudder and find his young pupils staring at him.

He looked for Susannah, only to find she had left Plymouth again for Exeter. The servants said she had gone back to Exeter to finish her schooling and might be away two years. Matthew brooded over his work and Combe looked at him often and shook his head. His mother worried but could think of no way of cheering him. Some days he wandered to the quays on some errand, real or imaginary, to stare at the ships in Sutton Pool, or farther afield to watch the ships at anchor in Turnchapel Bay. Though he would not admit it to himself, he was looking for Mary's father. What he would say to John Galton, if he did find him, Matthew did not know, but still he watched for that scarred face with its eye-patch, now so familiar to him, waking or sleeping.

Hawkins and his friends were gathering a new fleet. He had been to London, where his father-in-law, Benjamin Gonson, was Treasurer to the Queen's Navy. The news of Hawkins's last successful voyage to the Americas had gone before him and the word in Plymouth was that the Queen herself was giving her blessing to his next venture.

"Blessing," muttered Combe. "She has given that rogue more than her blessing and will get back even more."

Combe was right. A few days later, lying along with the Hawkins ships in the Cattewater, was a great vessel that towered over the rest, with its huge, gilded stern-castle. From the sailors on the *Romule* Matthew learned that this was the *Jesus of Lubeck*, a Crown vessel of six hundred tons. If the *Jesus* sailed with Hawkins's fleet, then that fortunate man had the Royal blessing and more.

"Heaven help him if he bring back less than twofold," growled Combe to himself as he paced moodily round his shop.

Once again the sprucely dressed John Hawkins came to the Morten home and this time took a glass of wine with Jacob. That Sunday, said Hawkins, there would be three hundred men, no less, in church for the farewell service. He would have young Matthew read the lesson, if Morten pleased.

Morten was not pleased.

"These days, Mr Hawkins, the Lord has given back to me my voice and I may read the lesson with ease."

Hawkins frowned. "The men did say to me that they would have the lad speak the verses – as he did before the last voyage."

Jacob's face clouded and Mistress Morten said hastily. "See, Jacob, let us order it so. Matthew shall read the lesson and thou speak a prayer."

"You are truly a wise woman, Mistress Morten," smiled Hawkins. "Let it be so. Here's my hand on it, Jacob, and with it a token of my pleasure – and you'll hear more of that on Sunday."

Matthew, behind the table in the shadowy corner of the room, thought he saw something pass between Hawkins and his father. But the movement was quick and discreet and he could not make it out. But on Sunday, after the service, as the sailors bore Jacob Morten's stretcher out into the churchyard, there was no mistake. One of John Hawkins's stewards approached and with some familiarity bent down, addressed Jacob as "Right-Hand" and dropped a small leather bag into his lap. Matthew's father speedily slipped it away, but Matthew had seen all quite clearly.

No sooner had the seamen laid down his father's stretcher in the kitchen and taken their leave when Matthew spoke out.

"Father, you took money from Mr Hawkins. You took payment for the service."

Jacob's eyes opened wider and his lips tightened. For a moment Matthew thought his father would deny what he had seen. But instead, Jacob merely answered lightly.

"And if a man do another service, may he not be recompensed? The labourer is worthy of his hire."

Matthew's voice shook.

"But the service is to the Lord You are not a hired priest in a nobleman's manor."

His father's head jerked forward. His voice took on that growling depth which Matthew had learned to fear in the past, though now he feared no longer.

"What, Matthew? You raise your voice against me? After what has passed?"

Matthew trembled. "Father, you did not lie in prison to take gold from rich men for prayer, to wear fine clothes . . ."

"And what of the clothes on your back, or your mother's for that matter? Do you believe they came out of nowhere?"

Matthew's voice now broke in his rage.

"You did say the Lord would provide, but you did not say in what manner it would be – a bag dropped in your fist by a gentleman's steward . . ."

"Matthew, Matthew," his mother's tearful voice interposed, but Matthew could not stop his rush of words.

"Men did tell me. Be proud that thou art the son of Jacob Morten, who did lie in jail so that all men might know the Lord's word in their own tongue."

Jacob stared. " 'Tis true and it has come to pass as the Lord willed it. We may worship Him in the true way."

"And doth the Lord will that one man shall have more prayers than another according to the length of his purse?" Matthew raged.

Jacob's voice was quiet but dangerous.

"John Hawkins is a godly man. Wherefore shall I not say his prayers? He hath laboured for the Lord and got great increase which the Lord hath blessed. They that sail with him have prospered."

"Aye," shouted Matthew. "They that did not perish of ship fever and other ills. And others will die on the voyage that is to come, despite John Hawkins's goodness . . ." Matthew hesitated as he saw the blood flood into his father's cheeks.

"Blaspheme not, Matthew Morten," roared Jacob. "It is in the hands of the Lord whether they live or die. I will pray that the Lord will be merciful . . ."

"And so he will be, but not according to how much gold John Hawkins's man drops in thy hand."

His father gave a choking groan, then raised his voice.

"Enough. Get thee gone, Matthew Morten. Take what thou hast and get thee from this house. A half-breeched 'prentice boy shall not sit in judgment on Jacob Morten."

He fell back, choking on the last words, chest pumping, mouth twisting, blood rushing to his face. Matthew turned and, covering his ears against his mother's cries to come back, ran at full stretch across the fields.

Down he ran, past the church, down Notte Street and out of the Hoe Gate. He ran so furiously that he did not see where he went till he was hard by the water at the Fisher's Nose bastion. The ferryman, pushing off on his way across the Cattewater, backed oars when he saw Matthew storm up to the jetty.

"Quick, Matthew lad. Thou must jump for it."

And without thinking, Matthew leapt the widening gap between jetty and boat and tumbled amid the feet of the half-dozen passengers.

"Why, 'tis Matthew Morten," said one. "Hast breath enough in thy body, after the service, for such haste?" The others laughed and made room for him. An old dame patted him on the cheek and told him he was a mortal fine Bible reader. Another passenger would have Matthew sing, but the ferryman declared that since church was over, Matthew should take his ease like any other Christian, and with that they left him alone.

At the other side he quickly separated from the other people and roamed off along the cliff tops to the heights to the south. There he lay down on the turf and gazed across the Sound, to the west, where Rame Head jutted out into the sea. Beyond lay the Channel and beyond that the wide sea, where in a few days' time Hawkins and his men would sail. The thought somehow soothed Matthew's anger and hurt. He went over in his mind the violent quarrel with his father. It amazed him, not by its violence, but by the fact that he had felt no fear. He realised that with fear of his father had gone respect, and that now both had vanished.

Or, had they really been disappearing, little by little, since his father had returned home?

Yet his father had a right to tell him to leave the house. If he despised the money he should despise the food and clothes it bought. Yet he could not take back those words. So he must make his own way somehow. He must leave home, leave Plymouth. And, if he left Plymouth, he wondered suddenly, would he roam from town to town in search of work?

And would the beadle come with his birch twigs and beat him out of town? "He that will not work, neither shall he eat." And would some young girl like Susannah take pity on his beaten back and throw him a coin or a crust?

As his thoughts ran on, so did the afternoon. The autumn sun that feebly warmed his back now dropped down towards the west. He raised his eyes to see a long golden path of sunlight stretching over the water. If only he could take ship and sail that golden way to the west.

"Have a care, young Morten, for that course will leave thee beached in Cawsand Bay."

Matthew leapt up in amazement. Had he thought aloud, or had someone read his thoughts? A few paces from the cliff edge a horse was grazing. Standing by and loosely holding the reins was Sir Henry Ferrers.

"Did I startle you? Bible reading and deep thoughts are bad for your wits. I'll wager that in his youngest days, I could never have crept up on your father like that, let alone ride up on horseback."

"I was thinking of . . ."

"You were thinking of sailing to the west, lad. No shame in that, though there's more honour eastwards, to my mind. Could you bear arms and be a soldier, Morten?"

"Why so, sir?"

"I'm newly home from Malta, lad. Next year there will be a great battle against the Turks. If it is won, then is Christendom safe. If it be lost, then nought can hold the Turk back. While this land calls down the wrath of God

51

upon the Pope and French Christians fight one another, the Turk advances. I would raise a troop, but every man jack has taken ship with Hawkins. 'Tis gold not glory that shines in their eyes."

He turned and stroked his horse's neck.

"Sir."

"Morten?"

"Sir, one day, outside the church, you jested with my father, and called him 'Right Hand'. When I asked my mother to tell me why, she would not."

Sir Henry threw back his head and laughed.

"I'll tell thee, lad. 'Twill do no harm. Jacob Morten first served with me as pikeman, when the Turks besieged Vienna. I was a young volunteer, with other Plymouth men. Some of them have grown too old and fat to remember. Of all the men in that army, none was stronger, none drank more deeply, cursed more lewdly, than Jacob Morten. No shame, thy father was a man. When he did stand upon the right hand, then the pikemen would never give way even when the foeman's horses trampled them. Thus men called him 'Right Hand'. When 'Right Hand' stood fast no man would flee.

"Thus have I known him nigh on forty years. When he took to the Bible and forsook cursing, I liked him none the less. When Queen Mary's men arrested him for peddling Geneva bibles, and he brake their heads for them, they threw him in jail. I rode to London to beg for his release, and lost my favour at court for it.

"Yet, since he returned, some light has gone out within him. Once he had fire in his belly, first for the Devil, and then for God. And now I cannot tell him apart from any black-backed merchant or clerk."

Sir Henry placed his foot in the stirrup and swung into the saddle. He looked down at Matthew.

"You have fire in your belly. Let it not die out."

With that he pressed in his heels and the horse carried him swiftly away.

Chapter eight

Matthew stood alone on the cliff top, gazing out to sea. But the golden gleam had faded from the water. The air grew chill. He turned and wandered moodily along the cliff edge towards Turnchapel Bay.

What to do now? Where to go? No use complaining that his father had driven him from the house, when he had long wanted to leave and only the thought of his mother had held him back. Where would he sleep that night? He could creep home and his mother could let him in through the little dairy door behind the kitchen. He could sneak upstairs and his father would never know. And, in the morning . . . no, that he would never do. Only children sneaked upstairs and prayed all would be well in the morning.

He reached the point, where the ferryman was making ready for the last journey of the day.

"There y'be, Matthew. Thy mother waits on the farther side. Poor soul, she feared y'd run away for ever."

Matthew leapt down into the boat, as the ferryman pushed away from the shore and out into the bay. The other side of the water was half lost in twilight. But he could see his mother waiting for him, the lanky figure of Old Tom at her side. The boat grounded and Matthew leapt out, bidding the ferryman good night. Then he clambered up to where his mother stood. She spoke quickly, before Old Tom could open his mouth.

"Matthew, lad," she took his hands. "I took thee for lost . . ."

His eyes grew hot. "Mother, didst think I would leave Plymouth and not tell thee?"

She breathed deeply: "I did not know. Thou wast so wroth. Like thy father in past days."

As they climbed the grassy slope towards the walls, Old Tom muttered: "I did bid the watch wait for us. Thou'rt a young hound, Matthew, to torment thy mother so."

"Hush, Tom," whispered Mistress Morten as they passed through the gate and bid the watch good night. "Matthew. Tom and his wife say thou shalt sleep with them tonight. Tomorrow we shall see."

Matthew thanked Tom and the old man wagged his head at him. They walked the distance home in silence.

Bad news travels fast and the morning brought an unexpected answer to Matthew's troubles. As he entered the shop, Abraham Combe was waiting for him.

"So you're the boy who'd read his father moral lessons, eh?"

Matthew did not answer but went to take up his leather apron.

"Eh, Matthew, what d'y say?" growled Combe.

Matthew paused with the apron strings in his hands.

"If you would set me off, Mr Combe, pray tell me and I'll go. But what has passed between my father and me, I'll not talk of to any man outside my home."

Combe smiled thinly. "No need, lad. 'Tis the gossip of the town – be thy cottage walls never so thick, they'll hear it at the Market Cross. Put thine apron on."

Matthew retied his apron. "Then you'll not set me off?"

"Not I. As thou sayest, 'tis thine own business. For my part, I'll not lose a good lad over someone else's quarrel. No advantage in that. See. I spoke privily with thy mother. There's a bed in the loft over the stable beyond the back court. Two meals a day in our kitchens, Sunday supper with us in the Broad Chamber. That's if thou will have it."

"But my 'prentice lines did not include my keep."

"I know. 'Tis not for nothing. I'll have thee by me to give me a hand in the evenings. That's my side of it." He held out his large hand, and Matthew took it. "Mind, I do not say thou'rt in the right. But I'll say this, Matthew Morten. Hast chosen a hard row to hoe, to be so particular how thy father gets his money."

Matthew stiffened and looked Combe in the eye.

" 'Tis as God chooses, who be right."

Combe's eyebrows lifted.

"Ah, 'tis God's choice, then. Well, I'll say this, young Morten. Whom God chooses, let them be not proud. Let them be afraid." And with that, he clumped out of the shop.

Two nights later, after Matthew had moved his belongings into the loft over Combe's stables, Abraham called him.

"Tonight, I'll have thee on hand in the Broad Chamber. Sir Henry Ferrers joins me, with a few friends, for supper. Look not so wide-eyed, Matthew. Ferrers is not too grand to sup with a man of substance." And Combe grinned and slapped his own bulging belly.

A good hour before supper, though, Sir Henry arrived on his own and was brought up to the Broad Chamber, where he and Combe sat down to wine. Matthew brought up all the reckonings he had made on voyages out of Plymouth and Exeter – figures gained by a shrewd sifting of quayside and counting house gossip. These were laid on the table and Combe had Matthew wait to explain the figures, where needed.

"See, Sir Henry. Sixty per cent did John Hawkins take on that last voyage. Every man with a share was made rich by it. Last year Hawkins's income was double the sum spent by our Council. What he does, others can."

Sir Henry sipped his wine, shook his head: " 'Tis all sweet and beckoning, Combe. But you must know how little my estate amounts to. I'm one of the Ferrers who range abroad, not those who wax fat at home. I have mortgaged my lands, such as they are, to equip my troop to sail to Malta. I could not lay hands on a penny piece."

Combe shook his head.

"I admire your courage, Sir Henry, as does all Plymouth. If only you were so shrewd in your choice of venture. Where's the good for England in shipping soldiers to die in Malta?"

Sir Henry frowned.

"You speak plain, Master Combe. I likewise. Men in England care too much for trade, too little for the kingdom's honour, or, for that matter, of the fate of Christendom. If the Turk drives beyond Malta, then our common faith is doomed." He stressed the word "common". Combe shrugged.

"My faith hath nought in common with that of the princes of Spain and France. I'll tell thee this, and openly. 'Tis not Christendom that's in dispute in the Middle Sea."

Sir Henry's eyes widened.

'Nay," Combe went on. "Why do we pay so dear for silks and spices? Because Venice and her traders have a hand-grip on the trade. Not a yard of cloth, nor an ounce of cinnamon, but the Venetian has his advantage. That is trade, not Christendom."

"Then," demanded Sir Henry, "you do not care if the Turkish fleet ranges the whole Middle Sea?"

"The Eastern princes have ruled those shores before and may do so again. But we may have the same goods and cheaper from the Americas."

"Trade, trade. I despise all your trading," Sir Henry burst out. But Combe grinned.

"Therefore is your estate sunk so low and your trade as soldier has become a burden."

Now it was Sir Henry's turn to grin. "A shrewd thrust . . ."

Combe seized his chance. "Trade and soldier must pull together, else both are ruined. The true enemy of England's trade is not the Turk, but Spain. You fight the Turk today. But tomorrow we must fight Spain."

56

"I trow not, Combe."

"Mistake me not, Sir Henry. I have no lust to fight the Don. Trade's sweeter than war to me. But 'ere many years, this way of our Queen and her court with Spain – kiss one day, scratch the next – must change. Spain's realms in the Americas want goods. We can supply them. Trade we must, or there'll be war."

Combe leaned over and filled Sir Henry's glass.

"So, what do you say to my little plan?"

Sir Henry was puzzled. "I have told you, Combe. I have nought to buy even a quarter or half of a quarter share in the meanest vessel."

"Nay, Sir Henry. But if you were in along with Abraham Combe and his friends, others might venture, out of respect for you, men who otherwise would hesitate."

"Venture my name, you mean?"

"Your name is worth more than my purse," said Combe. Then as he saw Ferrers shake his head, Combe urged. "Sir Henry, what do you say to a quarter share in a ship to sail to Africa and the Americas, next year. And I'll advance two hundred pounds to help your present expedition."

Sir Henry stared. "For a shrewd man, that sounds like madness to me."

Combe roared with laughter till his chins shook. "I value your name more than you do yourself."

Sir Henry's eyes narrowed. "You have more up that wide sleeve of yours, Abraham Combe . . ."

Combe's fat face grew bland. "You are shrewd enough to be a trader. Now what I have in mind concerns both your name, your family, and mine."

Suddenly, Combe turned and saw Matthew. "Be off with you, lad. Thanks for thy help."

Chapter nine

Next day, Matthew went down to the Cattedown, where a crowd of men and women had gathered to see Hawkins's fleet raise anchor and move out into the Sound. *The Swallow*, with Hawkins himself on board, led the way, while the Queen's ship, *Jesus of Lubeck*, dwarfing all the rest, brought up the rear.

"A fine-looking vessel, the *Jesus*," said a young gentleman.

"Rotten with timber worm," growled a voice in the crowd.

"Idle gossip, fellow," retorted the young man.

"I have sailed on her and on more ships than thou hast drunk glasses of wine," came the rough response. The crowd began to laugh and the young man flushed. But disdaining a quarrel, he turned his back.

"Well, John Galton, it may be as thou sayest," said a merchant in the crowd. "But if the *Jesus* be so foul a vessel, how will she keep station with the others – they being such handy craft?"

"Because John Hawkins does make it a rule that all his ships shall keep good company, stay close together in all weathers."

Another man laughed and spat into the water. "Since thou be so wise in John Hawkins's ways, Galton, why dost thou not steer his ship this voyage?"

"Because John Hawkins has other rules – prayers twice a day and no dicing on board . . ."

"And which did thou offend against?"

"Both." The crowd laughed.

"I came late to prayers but once. I had served two watches at the wheel in foul weather and slept so deep I heard not the call."

"And the dicing?"

"Ha. Prayers will keep a man in good heart in stormy weather, but they'll not pass the time when you be becalmed."

Amid more laughter the crowd began to disperse. Matthew, who had stayed quietly at the back, now stepped forward in front of the speaker. It was the lean man with the scarred face and eye-patch who had terrified Susannah and him that day in Breton-side when poor Mary died.

"John Galton . . ."

Galton turned and stared at Matthew.

"Aha, 'tis young Morten."

"You know me then?"

"For sure. I have heard you read and sing on Sundays. A fine voice." He stared at Matthew. "Why so amazed, lad? I go to church like any Christian. I'm no heathen. Even though John Hawkins did turn me off as a blasphemer after ten years in his service."

"Nay, forgive me," said Matthew. "That was not my meaning."

"Come with me for a cup of ale, then, lad, and tell me thy meaning."

Galton led the way back to Sutton Pool and the Golden Fleece, favourite of all who gathered at Custom Quay, worker or idler. As they walked, Matthew summoned up courage to speak again.

"Your daughter Mary was a sweet girl, and a dear friend to me."

John Galton's face darkened and his single eyelid drooped. "Aye. And your mother was good to my little ones when I was away at sea. Would to God I were at sea now, for I wander round by day and night and think of them all the time."

They entered the tavern and found a quiet corner. Galton called for ale.

"Sometimes I think God's curse is on me, for I brought the fever back with me from New Spain, but I did not die. Instead my wife and little ones did, every one.

"One day I was a happy homecomer with a belt full of silver. Ten days after I was alone. My money I gave to those of my shipmates' families that had need of it."

Galton drank deeply and looked from one fierce eye at Matthew.

"Argosies from the west bring advantage to some, and some only. Still, lad, thou hast not sought me out to hear my complaints."

"When I taught little Mary, she did tell me many things you said to her."

"Aye, poor soul. She thought all John Galton's grumbles and heresies were pure golden wisdom."

"And she learned fast."

"And you taught her well. 'Ere she died she talked of you all the time. That day, when you came with proud Susannah Combe, I was in a rage of despair. My heart was so full of hate. Afterwards I meant to seek you out and beg pardon. For I knew you had not come to pry, but out of friendship. Thou at least . . ."

"But Miss Susannah also . . ."

"Maybe. But she's a proud creature." Galton cocked an eye at Matthew's reddening face. "No matter. Now we have met, Matthew Morten, we shall be friends, I trust." He held out a lean, brown hand.

"Gladly," said Matthew.

"My Mary did tell me that you read Latin."

Matthew nodded.

"Then canst thou teach me? There are books with hidden wisdom . . ."

"I'll teach thee what I know willingly," said Matthew, "but where may we meet for our studies?"

"Not in the alehouse, for sure, or Abraham Combe will believe you a drunkard, and my drinking companions will believe me mad. Nay, come, when you may, to my lodging. I have a place with an old woman near the Dung Quay. Come, 'tis a step away, no more. I'll show you where it lays."

They left the alehouse and strolled to John's tiny room. He laughed. " 'Tis not easy on the nose, this place, but the old dame charges me little, and I have my ease."

He gripped Matthew's hand again.

"In return, is there ought I can teach you? A foolish question, perhaps . . ."

Matthew hesitated. A thought had sprung into his mind.

"Go on, lad. If it be in my power . . ."

"I have no skill in arms, neither with bow, staff nor sword . . ."

"But hast no need of them."

"But I would learn."

"Then, what I know, I'll teach you willingly," said Galton, mocking Matthew's solemn tone. And so they parted.

Through that summer, Matthew passed an hour with John Galton nearly every day. Only when Galton was hired as helmsman for a coastal voyage did they fail to meet. And each time, Matthew waited impatiently for John's return.

Early mornings, when it was barely light, Matthew would leap from his bed above the Combes' stable and creep out through the back gate. He would run to the Hoe to meet John Galton. Sometimes the sea-wind cut like a knife, but John would make him strip to the waist.

"Off with thy shirt, Matt. If I make thee bleed, twill spoil."

Then they would set to. Half of the hour they would fight with cutlass or sword, for John kept a small armoury, trophies from fights at sea. Half of the hour they would fight with quarter staff, or wrestle. Matthew found the going rough at first. It was hard to explain his bruises to his mother, or Mistress Combe. But John would give him no respite.

"Matthew, lad. No fancy work. I'll teach thee to fight as the forecastle fights. Not for sport, like the court gallants, nor for glory, but for dear life. For if it comes to close quarters at sea, when you hang on your foe's ratlines by your very teeth, and he'll have your blood, then, by God, you must have his blood and first. So, no time for salutes and courtesies, crossings of blades and hands on hips. Strike home."

And with this he would lunge savagely and Matthew would flinch, or leap aside, or, unbalanced, fall on his back, while John stood over him, blade raised. "Now, I have thee, Matt. Wriggle like an eel or I'll split thee. For thy life, now."

Early morning exercises and his own growth made Matthew ravenous. Mistress Combe would eye his emptied platter with amazement. Matthew would often slip home to his mother, in the quiet hour of the late afternoon while his father slept. There he would eat another meal and talk with her. He told her of his friendship with John Galton. He hid some of the details from her, but he suspected that she knew. From her sad looks he could tell that she felt he was growing away from her.

When Combe had no call for his work, Matthew would stroll round to John's lodgings for a cheerful hour. Half this time would be spent in teaching John Latin. And half would be spent in eating pies Matthew brought from home, drinking wine, and in talk. Matthew listened eagerly to John's tales.

"When you clear the Channel, Matt, the nor'easters carry you along, twenty, thirty, forty leagues a day. It grows warmer and you must watch your back, 'ere you lose a skin or two from the sun. The heavens are blue, the clouds fly and the sun goeth down like a ship on fire.

"When the Canaries lie astern then you set course for the Americas, with the easterly trades as your friend, you see the strangest beasts of the sea, shoals of squid like twisting shadows, flying fish on the water like pebbles skimmed over a mill-pond by a boy; they fly from the sea in terror when dolphins pursue them.

"And some days no wind, not even the faintest breeze. Then are you happy to leave the forecastle and sleep on deck in your shirt. The air is so still and hot at noon it takes your breath. Then the crew prays in earnest for a breeze or a squall of rain to fill the buckets. Or prays for a sight of a frigate bird or tropic bird that shows the coasts of the Americas be not far ahead.

"But when you see the peaks of Guadeloupe or Martinique rise from the sea, you know the voyage nears its end. But keep course to the south. There are lands where men have gone on shore after water and the people there butchered and ate them. And without saying grace. But in other islands are the people gentle and friendly – though the Spaniards have villainously abused them. There are tall trees, golden sands, sweet springs, game afoot or on the wing . . ."

Then, as John saw a gleam in Matthew's eye, he could change tack and talk of storms that blew up and sucked ships into the deep like breadcrumbs, of winds that tore sails to ribbons and plucked seamen from the yards like flies.

"You'll sleep on bare boards in the fo'c'sle amid foul air. No straw to lie on for fear of plague or burning. Salt beef – foul before the salt came near it, hard biscuit and mouldy cheese. A gallon of beer a day, sour before the voyage is half done – poisoning your belly. And, if the master be mean, six men will eat the food of four."

"Yet men go back to sea," said Matthew.

"As well starve at sea, as rot on shore," said John. "And men do dream of a share in a rich cargo. Men do always dream, such fools they be. The sailor dreams of gold pieces, the apprentice doth dream he has married the master's daughter."

In the candlelight he saw Matthew go red. The lad's face grew angry.

"Why, sir, have I offended thee? Tomorrow on the Hoe, shalt thou have leave to baste my hide in payment," said John.

Matthew laughed. Embarrassed as he was, he knew that John was right. Behind his waking and sleeping dreams was one of Susannah. It was a full year now since she had been sent away to Exeter. After that ill-fated venture into Breton-side she seemed to draw closer to him. But he could not be sure of her feelings. She was proud, as John said, and her smile mocked. But he, too, was proud. And when she returned to Stillman Street she would be under the same roof. Suddenly he recalled the words of young Ferrers's friend.

"Ferrers does not despise thee, Morten, he hates thee. Bethink you where you work."

Charles Ferrers, son of Sir Henry Ferrers, envied Matthew Morten, merchant's apprentice. His spirits rose.

Then, as swiftly, into his mind came a picture of Abraham Combe and Sir Henry, bending their heads over their wine glasses . . . "it concerns our two families . . ." And again Matthew felt gloomy.

In September Hawkins's fleet sailed into port, laden with ivory and elephants' teeth, pearls and gold, hides and sugar. On the quays some spoke of sixty per cent profit. Others laughed, waved their arms and said, "Nay, one hundred and sixty." The *Jesus of Lubeck* had survived the voyage. So it seemed all would be well at court for Plymouth's richest son. "Richest man in the kingdom," said some. Others said the Queen would award him a coat of arms.

But there were other voices at court. The Ambassadors of Spain and Portugal arrived with complaints that Hawkins had used "force" against their colonies in New Spain and Africa.

John Galton laughed. "Maybe he did force them to trade,

but I'll wager they submitted cheerfully. Then they wrote lying letters home to clear themselves."

When news came that the Queen had rebuked Hawkins and made him put down five hundred pounds as a guarantee he would not sail again to the Americas, John Galton laughed even louder.

"Hawkins has given his word. For sure he'll not sail again this year. But his ships will. Mark my word."

John was right. Before the autumn had passed, a fleet backed by Hawkins and his friends, under Captain Lovell, sailed for Africa.

"Such is the word of a gentleman, backed by five hundred pounds," laughed John.

For Abraham Combe, though, it was no laughing matter. It was the talk of Plymouth that his plans to fit out an expedition had been held up for lack of a fit vessel. His friends whispered that Abraham was afraid Africa and the Americas would be swept clean before Combe's ship could clear Rame Head. But Combe went on with his planning, leaving Matthew to handle all the day to day affairs of the business. Before Matthew realised, winter had arrived. Dark mornings cut short his daily bouts with John Galton.

In the midst of all this, Susannah returned from Exeter. She swept into the shop, cheeks aglow from the cold, eyes sparkling. "I am here to stay," she told Matthew, "and shall do as I please – 'til Father makes known to me what place I have in his many plans."

Matthew stared. Could it be true that she knew nothing of her father's plans? Her eyes were alight with innocent mischief. Did her words have two meanings?

Two days later she asked Matthew to escort her on an errand to Kinterbury Street. She soon made it clear that this was simply an excuse to get out of the house. Her father was in a bad temper the whole day, while Mistress Combe watched her like a hawk, "for fear I shall do some wrong – though what I know not."

"Does Mistress Combe know that you asked me to walk with you?" asked Matthew, suddenly bold. Susannah laughed. "If a maid may not be escorted by her father's apprentice . . ." Then she turned and begged his pardon. "That was thoughtless chatter."

She danced in front of him, then stopped in his path.

"We are friends, are we not, Matthew? In the past I have made thee wroth, for I was young and foolish. But now I am grown wise, I trow."

Despite himself, Matthew laughed. Some weeks later, Susannah sent a giggling servant girl to bid him come to the Broad Chamber. Though it was December, the day had been warm and bright and the setting sun now shone redly through the window, where Susannah sat, bent over a tiny book. As Matthew came into the room she looked up, smiled gaily and held out the book to him.

"See, Matthew, a gift I had from my cousin in Exeter."

Matthew took it.

"Why, 'tis verse."

"Indeed. Is that wicked?"

Matthew blushed. "How can I say, till I read therein?"

"My mother knows for sure that a book is wicked, if there be verse in it. Matthew, as you be my friend, so sit down now and read for me."

"And, if thy mother do come in?"

"You shall look grave and I shall say it is an improving book."

"And will that be the truth?"

"Aye, by my faith. For when you do read for me I shall be much improved. Read on, sir. My pleasure is Sir Thomas Wyatt's poem on the forty-sixth page."

Matthew sat down by the window and took up the tiny book. Susannah leant nearer him and he began to read softly.

"They flee from me that sometime did me seek

"With naked foot stalking within my chamber

"Once have I seen them, gentle tame and meek . . ."

When the poem ended, Susannah who had listened with parted lips and eyes full on him, let out her breath and clapped her hands.

"Now, Matthew. Do you read another poem – of your own choosing."

"But I know none of them."

"Do but close the book, then, and open it once more and read no matter what it be."

Matthew opened the book again.

"My galley, charged with forgetfulnesse,

"Through sharpe seas in winter nights doth passe . . ."

As he finished and handed back the book, Susannah said, "Hast chosen a sad poem."

But Matthew did not reply. He was thinking of John Galton and his troubles.

"The starres be hid that head me to this pain . . .

"Drowned is reason that should be my comfort . . ."

But John's reason had never been drowned. Storm-tossed, but not drowned. He bade Susannah good night and left the room.

Next day Mistress Combe called him. In her hand Matthew saw the book of poems.

"I'll thank thee, Matthew Morten, not to leave thy book in the Broad Chamber."

He opened his mouth to deny, but she thrust it under his nose. At the top of the title page was neatly printed, "Matthew Morten, his book", and the date, 17th December, 1566.

He swallowed. "I beg pardon, Mistress Combe. I had forgot."

Later that day when Susannah tripped into the shop, he challenged her.

"Forgive me, Matthew," she said. "I feared that Mother might pry into what I read, but if she saw thy name she would look no further, for she knows thou dost read all manner of strange things!" She smiled. "Hast thou a pen?"

Matthew handed her his quill. She placed the book on the counter, wrote in it and handed it to him.

"There. 'Tis thine and no deceit." And she slipped quickly from the shop.

Matthew opened the book. Under his name was written: "From his friend, Susannah Combe."

Chapter ten

Spring brought a hard blow to Matthew's dreams. Sir Henry Ferrers rode back into Plymouth, bearing the ribbons of high foreign orders for his battles against the Turks. In church, the Sunday before Easter, Matthew, who sat now a little way apart from his parents, saw Sir Henry, splendidly dressed as ever; and next to him, the tall handsome Charles Ferrers down from Oxford. He saw young Ferrers eyeing the Combe family and for a moment their glances crossed in mutual hostility.

That evening the Ferrers came to supper in the Broad Chamber. Matthew was told to bring certain papers there and found Charles and his father with Combe. This time Matthew was dismissed straight away. As he went back to his rooms he heard the servants laying the table, and bit his lip in vexation. Slipping on his jacket, he left the house and ran round to John Galton's lodgings. John was newly home and gave him a cheerful welcome. He quickly saw that Matthew was out of sorts and pulled a bottle of wine from the bag beneath his bed.

Handing Matthew a glass, he said shrewdly, "Matthew, lad, if the race were equal, I'd lay all I own on thy success. But 'tis not equal. As thou well knowest, Charles Ferrers knows how to cut the corners and come in first. Well, thou hast three courses of action."

Matthew stared in astonishment.

John laughed: "One – forget proud Susannah.

"Two – slay Charles Ferrers.

"Three – become so rich even Abraham Combe will serve thee.

"Now," he continued, "the first course is out – I see by thy face. The second were sinful, unless Ferrers sought to slay thee first. So there's nought to it. Thou must become rich."

"But how?"

"Since thou wilt not do it by thy prayers – nay, Matthew, the whole town knows the cause of thy quarrel with thy father – then thou must do it by thy deeds. Take ship with Hawkins. Thy family is in his favour. And this year, they tell me, John himself will take a great fleet to Africa, with the Queen's blessing, her gold and half the men in Devon."

"How can I sail with Hawkins, if I am bound to Abraham Combe?"

"Ah," said John, sipping his wine. "Then, when Combe fits out his vessel, ship as his quartermaster. Thou'rt young, but few in this port can reckon better than thee. As quartermaster thou mayst cheat both master and crew, selling one short on the cargo and the others on the rations. In two voyages art thou made rich."

Both laughed, and Matthew went home in good spirits. Next day he discovered that John's information, as ever, was true. The Hawkins family were assembling their biggest fleet. The *Jesus of Lubeck*, as gilded and ramshackle as ever, was brought round from the Thames. There was the *Minion*, the *William*, the *John*, the *Judith*, the *Angel*, as well as the old *Swallow*.

Later that summer, the *Castle of Comfort*, captained by Lovell, sailed into Plymouth. The quayside taverns were full of her crew's adventures. It was said that young Drake, from Crowndale, a cousin of Hawkins, had put a shot through the governor's house at Rio de la Hacha – when that gentleman declined to trade with the English.

As the fleet assembled and the sailors gathered in Plymouth, the rumours grew. Hawkins was said to be bound for the fabled gold mines of Wangara, in Africa. When he heard this, John Galton, sitting with Matthew in the Golden Fleece, snorted with derision. The teller of the tale grew indignant.

"I tell thee, John Galton. All wisdom's not thine. I know for sure that two Portuguesers have come to London. They have secret maps that do show the way to a great hoard of both gold and silver. Jewels beside."

John Galton slapped the table and roared with laughter. "I can make thee a map that will show where the Grand Cham of Tartary doth hide his jewel-encrusted nightshirt and thou no doubt would give me a year's wages for it."

As laughter rang round the tables, the sailor flew into a rage. But John spoke calmly.

"Nay, lad, be not wroth. I'll tell thee how we may know for sure Hawkins is not bound for the Africa gold mines."

"How?" shouted half a dozen voices.

"Why is Hawkins lading his ships with horse beans? Will he trade them for gold. Eh? Let the first man of Hawkins on this table who will eat horse beans put up his hand. Nay, none of you would. Hawkins is loading horse beans to feed slaves. It is black gold he seeks in Africa, slaves to sell to the pearl fishers of Margarita and the plantation masters of Terra Firma. No trade is so rich as the trade in human flesh."

"Ah," said one sailor. "Haply thou'rt right, John Galton. Lovell did bring back a blackamoor on the *Castle of Comfort*. He roams the quayside and, God's wounds, he's an ugly creature, with a scar from chin to crown."

John thrust forward his own scarred face. "Why, dog, wilt thou say I'm ugly?"

The other took it with good humour. "Why, to be sure, John. But, be not envious when I tell thee, the blackamoor is ten times as ugly as thee. He be so ugly, men called him 'Satan'."

John joined in the laughter that spread through the room. A sailor shouted. "Where is this marvel? I'll wager two-pennorth of ale, my old shipmate John Galton is uglier than any blackamoor." Back came the answer, "Threepennorth of ale on Satan." The tavern was in an uproar, when a sailor ran in and bellowed.

"Hold your penny pieces and come out. Satan himself marches along the quay. Come out and we'll make a match."

In an instant, the tavern emptied and the sailors crowded out on to the jetty, where they mingled with Hawkins's men busy loading a vessel. Barrels and bales were overturned and there were curses on both sides. But all suddenly fell silent and turned to look along the quay.

"There be Satan himself. Judge now who be uglier."

Along the quay shambled a man. His leg bent out of true and he lurched to one side. This, combined with the sloping shoulders and lolling head, made him look like a crab. Under the ragged shirt the shoulders gleamed black and powerful. On he came, seeming not to notice the crowd.

"Come, Satan, show us thy face. Hold up thy head, Satan."

The black man halted at the shouts and held up his head. Matthew caught his breath. The scar, in the form of a V, rose from beneath his nostrils to his forehead, fanning out above the eyes to give his face a truly Satanic look. As Satan saw the jeering crowd, he lowered his face and turned.

But a man rushed forward. "Hey, Satan, do'ee but stand still a while, so we may see thy face."

The tone was good humoured, but the black man was in no mood to oblige. He set off up the quay with the sailor after him.

John Galton whispered in Matthew's ear.

"Mat. I smell trouble. Do but edge out of the crowd and stand with me by the warehouse wall, where the arms are stacked."

Matthew did as he was bid and they reached the wall by the arms barrels just as the sailor caught up with Satan, only a dozen paces away.

The man reached out in sport to clap his hand on Satan's shoulder. The black man turned, with grace and deadly speed. The sailor was seized round the waist, hoisted in the air and flung over the edge of the quay into the water.

"Now watch thyself, Matthew, for that was a Hawkins man," said Galton.

Out of the crowd charged a huge sailor, cutlass drawn. Halting lightly, left foot forward, he swung his blade and it seemed for a moment a second brutal scar would join the first on Satan's skull. But Satan leapt back, and drew from his rags a long curved knife. This swung up in a graceful arc, turning the cutlass blade aside. Satan feinted with his blade and a long rip showed in the sailor's shirt. Again the sailor swung his cutlass. Again came the riposte and this time his breeches were slashed. And again, the sailor's tam o' shanter was in ribbons. A fourth time and the cutlass flew from his grasp and stuck, quivering, in the ship's timbers.

Satan stood, breathing deeply, legs astride, as if inviting come-who-might to attack him. Three Hawkins men lunged forward, while two more sidled along the quay to take him from the rear.

"Now, Matthew," whispered John. The two snatched up cutlasses from the arms barrels.

"Satan!" called John. The black man's glance flickered round. "Over here by the wall." The black man hesitated but a second, then scuttled, crab-like, to the warehouse. John and Matthew ranged themselves on either side of him.

"Now," shouted John, "come one come all. But let the odds be even."

The other sailors hung back, but the Hawkins men sprang forward, blades at the ready. Matthew to the right, Satan in the centre, John to the left, met the thrusts of half a dozen cutlasses. Matthew felt a blade nick his arm, but saw his attacker fall back, his cheek red with blood. John had felled his man with the flat of his blade, Satan had disarmed his opponent. The three now, as one man, lunged forward at their remaining opponents.

But the air was split by the agitated ringing of an alarm bell and the cry, "The watch, the watch." Through the crowd marched the constables and, behind them, the elegant figure of John Hawkins.

"John Galton, by my word. I might have known," said Hawkins. "I did well to turn thee off."

"Mr Hawkins, sir," said Matthew. "Galton did but aid the blackamoor who was beset by four of your men."

"Ha. Jacob Morten's son. I see why thy father thrust thee out of doors." Hawkins turned to the watch. "Do your duty. Take these men for raising a riot."

"Nay, not so fast," spoke a commanding voice from farther along the quay. There stood Sir Henry and Charles Ferrers, the latter gazing in amazement at Matthew's grounded cutlass and bloodied sleeve. Abraham Combe stood by, his face furious.

"Why, Sir Henry," said Hawkins, "what would you?"

"I would that you should not touch these men."

"And why?"

"They are of the company of a ship, *The Golden Way*, owned by my partner Abraham Combe and me."

Chapter eleven

The men on the quay fell silent. Matthew could hear seagulls cry overhead and the flap of the standard on the ship's mainmast. Hawkins regarded Sir Henry coolly a moment, then smiled.

"Well, 'tis nought to me how you raise your crews, Sir Henry, Mr Combe. A psalm singer cast out of doors by his father, a heretic rogue and a blackamoor. I wish you joy of them. But if you plan to forestall me in the quest for African gold you must look sharp, for I shall sail within a week."

"Have no fear," said Abraham Combe. "We shall be off the Africa coast before your old tubs have cleared the Canaries."

Hawkins grinned.

"Then I must beg leave to go about my lading. I wish ye good day." He paused and eyed Matthew. "Art a chip off the old block, Morten. But oblige me by returning the blade, when thou hast cleansed it, to my arms cask."

At Hawkins's command the crowd broke up, the Hawkins men to their work, the idlers to their ale. John Galton took up a sack, drew the cutlass blade rapidly through it and flung the weapon into its cask. Matthew followed suit. Satan, his long knife stowed out of sight, sank down by the wall, head sunk on chest. John turned to Abraham and Sir Henry.

"So, we are imprest into your service, sirs?"

"Nay," said Abraham, "art free to go with the watch."

"Then I'll bid ye good day, Matthew, I'll see thee anon." And he strode away down the quay.

"Wait," called Sir Henry. "Not so fast, Galton. 'Twas a jest. If this riot had not passed, I would still have wished that John Galton, best helmsman in Plymouth, should make one of the company. Come, man, 'twill be sevenpence a day, sixpence in harbour."

Abraham looked askance at Sir Henry, but said nothing. John walked back to them.

"Done. But for two things."

"Name them."

"What terms for my shipmates?"

Abraham intervened. "The boy is my 'prentice, the black-amoor a runaway. They'll get their keep."

"Not so," said John. "If ye sail not with the ship's company, the lad's training is not in your hands. He will be a deck-learner, perhaps even have charge of the ship's store. He'll rate his fivepence a day. And I fancy Satan will be worth his weight in gold when we heave to off Senegal."

"Senegal? Who says we sail for Senegal?"

"Abraham Combe. I have been to sea for thirty years. I know how the wind sits from the shape of the cloud. You no more fool me than Hawkins does with your talk of gold-mines. I've seen your ship in Turnchapel Bay. She's no flier, but strong, and will stand a gale – better than that gilded hulk out there," he jerked his thumb over his shoulder. "But she was built with a side-hatch and ramp for shipping soldiers. I trow you'll use her for slaving."

"And . . ."

" 'Tis a trade for Turks, not Christian men."

"Ah, the heretic moralises," rumbled Abraham. "Ask Matthew what the Book says. What did Noah say of Canaan, son of Ham?"

Matthew was silent, head down. John said: "Go to, Matthew, what does the Bible say?"

"Cursed be Canaan. A servant of servants shall he be unto his brethren," Matthew muttered.

"A truce to this Scripture-citing," broke in Sir Henry. "Galton, we accept thy terms for thee and thy shipmates. If thou likest not the voyage, then go thy ways."

John eyed Sir Henry levelly. "My heart saith nay, my empty purse saith yea."

He turned to go, then paused. "That ship was the *Providence* out of Fowey, I believe. But ye have renamed her."

Sir Henry smiled. "Aye. She's called *The Golden Way* after a fancy of young Morten's here."

John nodded. "Satan and I will have our gear aboard *The Golden Way* 'ere nightfall. Hopefully thy name is a good omen."

He tapped Satan lightly on the shoulder. The two disappeared among the crowds along the quay. Sir Henry and Charles, who had stood restlessly by through the whole conversation, now took their leave. Abraham glowered at Matthew.

"Well now, we must see to altering the terms of thy apprenticeship. Galton is a shrewd fellow. It was in my mind to bid thee ship as quartermaster. I know thou'rt fit for it, young as th'art. First, we'll to Stillman Street."

As they walked up to the Combe house, came the distant sound of cannon fire. Matthew supposed the ships were firing at target. But Abraham, mystified, shook his head. "That came from the Cattewater, if my ears deceive me not. Something's afoot, and I'll wager that man Hawkins is behind it." Matthew hid a smile and busied himself in the shop.

Soon a servant rushed in excitedly. Spanish ships had attacked the fleet and Hawkins's men had beaten them off. Combe grimaced. "Battle. No more than five shots."

But later, Charles Ferrers arrived on a courtesy call and told another story:

"Flemish ships, under Baron Wacheren, so I'm told, on

their way to the Spanish realm in the Low Countries. As they came round the point they did neither dip flags nor strike foresails to show peaceful intent. Hawkins asked no questions but put shots in their sides. Now, so I hear, the Baron is in town complaining to the Lord High Admiral's men. He says they were in haste to shelter from bad weather. But Hawkins has told the mayor . . ."

"A bosom companion of his," grunted Abraham.

". . . that he suspects the Flemish ships want to hinder his expedition to Africa."

Abraham nodded. "That has a ring of truth. Well, may they hinder him. Come, Charles, we'll to the ladies."

Matthew worked swiftly and had finished by late afternoon. He put on his jacket and walked slowly home across the fields. As he hoped, his father slept, his well-curled beard rising and falling over his well-starched collar. The face was gentle in sleep and Matthew thought to himself, "I am a fool to quarrel with him. I should go my own way."

He persuaded his mother to walk with him up the hill. The air was fresh and still warm, though the year turned to the autumn. Walking arm in arm over the grass, Matthew found it easier to tell his mother what had happened. To his relief she was calm. Only a certain lowness in her voice betrayed her sadness.

"I knew thou must leave us, Matthew. But I am glad thou hast a good friend in John Galton."

Matthew nodded, his heart lighter.

"But, Matthew, I'll ask thee but one thing, 'ere thou goest."

"Mother?"

"That thou come and ask thy father for his blessing."

"I will, but will he give it?"

"Let me but speak with him first."

"As thou wilt, Mother. I do it but for thee."

"Thou judged him hard, Matthew. He is an old man and needs comfort in his latter years."

"I cannot unsay what I said, Mother. Let God judge between us."

She looked at him.

"Well, thou art indeed grown a man, Matthew."

That evening Matthew went with fresh-baked pies to John Galton's lodging. To his astonishment, it was crowded. Eight men sat around on John's pallet or on the floor. Among them were Hawkins's men, two bearing the marks of the morning's battle at the quay.

"Art amazed, Matthew, lad?" said John. "Here, squat down. Pass round thy pies and take a glass of wine. These are old shipmates. 'Twould take more than a fight to make us foes. But see, even Satan has forgiven and forgotten!"

Satan's deep eyes in his twisted face gleamed in the candlelight, motionless, but watchful.

"We have a purpose, Matthew, close to your heart. We would have you with us," said John. "Those Flemish ships do sail in the Spanish King's service. Aboard are prisoners, Protestants who will serve neither Philip nor the Pope. Can we allow them to stay captive, in sight of a Protestant port?"

"Nay," said Matthew.

"We eight shall venture out this night, with two boats, one borrowed of Combe, the other of Hawkins. We've not told them lest they fret. We need a handy lad to climb aboard, raise the hatch and bid the Flemings come up and away with us.

"Wilt thou be that lad?"

"Aye," breathed Matthew. "Right gladly."

Chapter twelve

The two boats moved out from the Cattewater until they picked up the current from the river, flowing strongly with the ebb tide. Here the flow of the water carried them down in the darkness past the silent, shadowy hulls of Hawkins's ships and away into the Sound, where the Flemish ships lay.

"Art ready, Matthew, lad?" whispered John.

"Aye."

Quickly, the shape of the Flemish flagship loomed up in the darkness. Strong arms reached out to fend off the small boats to starboard and larboard. As yet no noise. Only the ships' lanterns flickered in the night breeze.

"All asleep, I'll wager," muttered one man.

"Quiet," hissed John, and signalled to Satan who rose, straddling the gently rocking boat, and made a step for Matthew with his clasped hands. Matthew put his foot between them and felt himself rise effortlessly above Satan's shoulders. With two quick heaves on the cat-ropes, Matthew found a handhold at the angle between poop-deck and quarter-deck rail. No one about. A few quick strides and he was down the companion way. There was the watch, a bent figure at the rail of the half-deck, gazing out to sea. A movement forward caught Matthew's eye, though the Flemish sailor saw nothing. A dark shape rose from the ship's side and melted into the rigging. It was Satan for sure, and Matthew felt a surge of courage.

Barefoot, he stole across the half-deck. No movement from

the watch. Slowly he swivelled round and lowered himself down the steps. Half-way down he stopped dead and pressed himself flat against them. Boards creaked above him as though the watch were prowling. Then all was quiet. Matthew was on the main-deck.

The hatches were open a handsbreadth to give air to the prisoners, but they were secured. Matthew looked up. He could see the white of the sailor's face looking down. Heart thumping, he crouched into the angle between hatch and deck and willed the man to move. Then he took courage again and slid on his stomach around the hatch to put it between himself and the watch. There he began the delicate business of easing back the fastenings. They moved slowly, but easily. Now for the other side. If only the man would turn seaward again. But he could wait no longer. He must attempt the other side whatever the risk.

Sliding round the hatch once more, he tackled the fastenings on the starboard side. At first they would not budge. The sweat poured from him. His fingers bled. But the bolt slid back. Now speed was the main thing. He turned on his back to press upward on the edge of the hatch cover – and looked straight into the startled eyes of the Flemish seaman.

In that second, as the man hesitated between leaping on Matthew and raising the alarm, a great shadow flitted from the rigging like a bird. A black arm rose and fell. The stunned watchman was lowered to the deck and Satan helped Matthew fling back the hatch cover. Matthew leaned over. There were stirrings below.

"Come up, friends. Come up."

More stirrings. A head and shoulders loomed up over the edge. Round, half-asleep eyes regarded Matthew in bewilderment. Matthew gestured wildly to the side of the ship.

Now the man had his meaning. He heaved himself over the edge on to the deck and scampered where Matthew's finger pointed. Another man followed, and another, running now to starboard, now to larboard.

But the silence was broken. Excited scufflings could be heard as men struggled up to the hatch opening, scrapings and bumpings as they rushed to the side and swarmed over. Lights flashed in the forecastle. Men shouted and appeared on deck – one, two, three.

"Quick, Satan," called Matthew.

Satan hauled up the last prisoner, then ran to one side of the deck, while Matthew ran to another, confusing the crew men who ran towards them. Matthew paused a fleeting moment to allow the last prisoner over the side. Then he swung his leg over the ship's rail. In that instant he saw a sailor rush at him. A blade flashed. A moment's raking pain as the cutlass point scored the back of his thigh and he was free, over and falling down into the sea.

He plunged below the surface and rose, spluttering and kicking. He was grabbed and hauled into Galton's boat, and as the alarm rang out and lights showed all over the flagship, the two boats, laden with escaped prisoners, were heading for the shore.

"They'll not dare lower boats now. Heave away, lads. If trouble comes, 'twill be tomorrow."

He was right. Morning found the town in a ferment. Baron Wacheren and his lieutenants were on shore at first light. The mayor and Lord Admiral's man were fetched from their beds. A great search was made of taverns and ware-houses. The watch even made a half-hearted attempt to search the hovels of Breton-side, but were driven off by a shower of dirt and stones by the Breton boys. But Baron Wacheren declared that he would either have his captives back or he would see the raiders punished.

Soon enough the search led to John Hawkins's house on Kinterbury Street. It was he who had bombarded Wacheren's ships. But Hawkins met the Baron, mayor and their party with a courteous dismissal.

"If men had boarded my ships at night, they would not have got away. If you cannot show me more than mere guesswork, I cannot help."

By mid-afternoon the party, now swelled by other officials, had reached the Combe house in Stillman Street. By now the Baron's patience was wearing thin.

"Sir, I have made formal complaint to London. If the men I seek are in your pay, I request you to hand them over to the Lord Admiral for punishment."

Combe pursed his tiny lips.

"Even if my men did raid your ship to set free Protestant captives, and I do not say they did, I shall hand over no man. My ship waits to sail and I'll not have it delayed by courts of inquiry."

The Baron's eyes narrowed: "So your ship will sail with guilty men on board? Have a care, sir. Bold words in Plymouth Town may not sound so bold on the high seas."

Combe stared. "You intend . . ."

"I say no more. I ask your help in a matter of justice."

"Hm," said Combe. "Well, then. Show me if one of my men be guilty and then we'll see."

"Good. The men from my flagship say that they saw men leaving in two boats. One of the raiders was a lad of no more than sixteen."

"There's more than one in Plymouth," grinned Abraham.

"Ah," replied the Baron, "but this lad was nicked by a cutlass point as he fled. It should not be too hard to find the boy."

"Come, sir," said the Lord Admiral's man. "Call up your servants and let us cast an eye over them."

When Matthew entered the Broad Chamber with the servants the room seemed full of richly dressed officers. Combe, he noticed, looked nervous. A severe, black-clad man who sat by the table suddenly fixed his eye on Matthew, whose heart sank.

"Ah, you have one lad of sixteen years."

"Indeed," said Combe. "A worthy lad, known throughout Plymouth for his bible-reading. Not a likely raider."

"He might do so to free companions of his faith," said the man in black. And he barked at Matthew.

"Turn around, young man."

Unthinking, Matthew turned. The Baron's man leapt forward and pointed. Down the back of Matthew's breeches ran a jagged tear. It parted to show a cut with the blood freshly clotted.

Matthew jerked round again. The man in black was smiling grimly. "Well, sir," he said to Abraham. "What do you say? Is he our ship raider, or not?"

"No, sir, he is not."

The quiet clear voice came from the open door. The Baron rose and bowed. In the doorway stood Susannah, pale face framed in chestnut hair. She stepped forward and confronted the Baron.

" 'T'would be an injustice, sir, to punish a young man for aiding his master's daughter."

Combe stared. Matthew looked at the floor.

"This morning," went on Susannah, "my bonnet blew into a bush. This lad did bring it down for me and tore breeches and flesh."

"And this you did see?" asked the Baron.

"I give you my word," said Susannah.

"Thank you," said the Baron. And to Combe. "Sir, I'll trouble you no longer." He moved to the door, his officers following.

As he passed Matthew, he said:

"Lucky man, to have a maid to give her word for you. May you do as much for her when she hath need of it."

And with that he was gone.

Chapter thirteen

For all his strivings and his grumblings, Combe could not get *The Golden Way* ready before Hawkins's ships sailed. The Sunday before, five hundred Hawkins men gathered in church. Matthew could see the ill humour on Combe's vast white face as he glared at them.

But he could do nothing. Three of his crew had fallen sick – captain, boatswain and a deck hand. For several days Combe had been searching ports throughout Devon and even in Cornwall to find men to replace them.

Matthew had made his peace with his father and sat by his side while Jacob read the lesson. Jacob read with force but still his voice did not carry, and some at the back of the church who could not hear were plainly restless. Matthew's eyes ranged the congregation. His past life was there, in their faces.

The wrinkled, irritable, kindly face of Old Tom: "Nay, fret not, lad, I'll see thy mother well."

Abraham Combe's glowering face. "If this venture go well, Matthew, there'll be a partner's share, albeit a small one, in my next voyage."

Mistress Combe, straight and severe: "Art a strange lad, Matthew. We shall miss thee, but this is for the best."

Susannah, fresh and lovely in dark velvet: "God go with thee, Matthew Morten, and keep thee safe from harm. Now I must read my poems to myself."

Sir Henry Ferrers, hawk-eyed and splendid: "Had I my

way I'd take thee with me when I set out. Jacob Morten came with me on my first. 'Twould be good to have his son with me on my last expedition."

"Last, Sir Henry?"

"Aye, Morten. I'll be in my dotage. But thou shalt come and tell me sea-tales."

Charles Ferrers, now as tall as his father, as arrogant but without his humour. He was to sail to Malta with his father. He had nought to say to Matthew and Matthew returned the compliment.

And Matthew's mother, small face now more lined, blue eyes more faded. She had no more to say. But when Jacob came to the words, "He bringeth them into their desired haven," she took Matthew's hand and pressed it.

Then the day came when Matthew stood with John aboard *The Golden Way* in Plymouth Sound.

"Here come the rest of the crew," he said.

John Galton looked closely at the approaching boat, where Abraham Combe sat with three other men.

"Aha," he said, half to himself. "Skipper Tregarron of Fowey, and the brothers Churler from Bideford. One righteous, two wicked, and all three hard men."

"Are they good seamen?"

"If we must sail under a Cornishman, I'd as lief sail under Tregarron as any. As to Harry and Ben Churler, they know their business. 'Tis when they mix in other's that they must be watched."

As the boat drew under the stern, Matthew could see the men more closely. Tregarron the skipper was a dark, gloomy man, with a nose like a hatchet blade and thick black eyebrows above it. By contrast, the Churler brothers were short, fat and jolly, red faced, their features ringed with flaming red hair. As they came over the side, swinging their sea-bags, they looked like two small suns rising from the sea. They had hearty, boisterous voices, and when they were together would look to one another and say:

"Be that not right, Harry?"

"That it be, Ben."

So alike were they Matthew thought they must be twins. But John Galton doubted it. "God could not curse one mother with two such sons in the same day," he said.

Matthew was puzzled at John's dislike of the Churlers who seemed amiable enough. When the crew were gathered on the main-deck to meet the new skipper and boatswain, the difference in manner between Tregarron and Ben Churler was striking.

Tregarron made himself clear.

"Hear ye, men. 'Twill be a long time before we sight Rame Head again. We be twenty-five to sail *The Golden Way* to Africa, New Spain and back. Some say we sail short-handed. I'll not deny there'll be less lolling in the sun. But 'tis a golden rule, the fewer the men, the less the fever, and with God's help we shall see England again in good health and with full pockets."

Tregarron silenced the cheer that started.

"With God's help, I do say. And that means in God's way. Twice a day the bos'n shall read prayers before the main mast. Let none be absent. Ye know the penalties. I'll allow no blasphemy, filthy talk, dicing nor carding. Ye know the penalties. Now to your quarters. We sail on the dawn tide."

Tregarron went to one side with Abraham Combe, and Ben Churler beckoned the men to gather round him.

"I do have no fancy talk, but my ways will be known to ye soon enough. Those that be slow to learn shall be helped on their way, cheerfully." Churler flicked idly at his leg with a rope end which appeared in his hand as if by magic.

"Be that not right, Harry?"

"That it be, Ben."

"Now, fellows, stow gear and be merry. In the morn we do start with a will," and the bos'n sauntered away to doff his cap to the departing Abraham Combe. Combe called Matthew and the lad joined him where he chatted to

Tregarron. Churler, tam o' shanter in red fist, stood by.

"Tregarron. Here ye have Matthew Morten, quarter-master. Aye, I know he's young and it's his first voyage. But he has a rare head for figures. What's more, Churler, the lad will take the burden of prayer reading from thy shoulders. His reading and singing are beloved in all churches."

"Aye," said Tregarron. "I did know of his father. He shall read the lessons . . ." he seemed to catch Churler's eye, "in the evening, while the bos'n shall say prayers in the morning. And if Morten keep count of stores and cargo even as he read the lesson, he and I shall not fall out. But, quarter-master, lessons or no, every man on this vessel shall haul when the wind blows. Be that understood, Morten?"

"Aye, sir," said Matthew, and turning to Combe, he bowed and said, "Do but give my respects to Mistress Combe and Susannah, master."

Combe's face softened. "God go with thee, Matthew. Keep well my cargo. Much hangs on its homecoming."

Matthew went forward to the forecastle. As John Galton had warned him, crew's quarters were simple – a space on the deck-planking. He and John had marked out their places early, "Where we may get air to breathe, but not take chill by night," said John. Matthew arrived to find Harry Churler about to push his gear to one side. His anger flared.

"There is room enough for all. No need to take my place," he said.

Churler straightened his back, the red face a picture of good humour.

"Ah, but a boy don't need the place of a grown man. And I be on the larger size." Some of the crew laughed.

"Then let thy largeness wax on the starboard side and not on mine," replied Matthew, and pushed his gear back into place.

"Nay," said Churler gently. "My place shall lie here. Let us not quarrel, lad, but be friends. 'Tis ever my way."

"Aye," came a level voice from behind Churler. "Art a

reasonable fellow, Harry Churler. None more so. And so, for that matter, be young Matthew. But if he do sweetly give way to thee, he must shift to larboard and take from my place. And I am a most unreasonable man."

The grin on Churler's lips drooped a little, then revived.

"Why, 'tis John Galton, on my life. The best helmsman 'twixt here and Land's End, if there be no Cornishmen in this fo'c'sle to take offence. And ever ready with a jest. Thou'd not take offence over a small matter like a boy's space?"

"Ah, Harry. Years have passed since we two sailed together and I fear I'm changed for the worse. Ill temper is my way, and quick to flare, unhappily. So, good fellow that thou art, do but shift thy carcass to starboard."

Churler's grin remained. Without a word he stowed his gear a good pace from Matthew's. Galton signalled to Matthew and the two went out on the foredeck. The sun was down, but a faint greyness hung over the sea and the lights of Plymouth Town twinkled like stars.

"I'll give thee good advice, Matthew, lad. Beware Churler, and more so beware the bos'n, his brother. Thy wrath is such that thou wilt be in scrapes 'ere we clear the Channel. I took thy part in this for I would not see thee outfaced before the voyage had begun. But if thou wilt defy a bully boy, be sure thou hast the weight to see thee through the engagement, before thou fire the first shot."

"Thou'rt a true friend, John," said Matthew, gratefully. "And I do thank the day that brought us together."

"Hey, Matthew, lad. We shall see good times and bad, together, 'ere we see these lights again."

"Will it be a good voyage, think you, John?"

Galton shrugged. "If Abraham Combe has his way, 'twill not be far short of five thousand pounds' return. And that can mean twenty pound for all who come safely home."

"More than a man might earn in three years," said Matthew. "And Abraham Combe has promised me a small partner's share in his next venture, if all go well this time."

"Well he might," said John drily. "Hast still dreams of wealth and a fortunate match, Matthew?"

Matthew reddened. "I will work and hope."

John gripped Matthew's shoulder. "Labour thou will that is certain sure. Hope, too, is thy birthright. But the outcome is unsure."

"How so, unsure?"

"Matthew, lad. We two are shipmates. I'll speak plain. Dost think thou canst carry off Susannah under Charles Ferrers's nose?"

"She has looked on me kindly."

John shook his head.

"Those who love are blind, 'tis true. But 'tis all arranged. Combe lends money for Ferrers's soldiering. Ferrer lends his name to this venture. Quid pro quo, as the scholars do say, or as we simple folk have it. You scratch my back, I'll scratch thine."

Matthew shook his head, bewildered.

"Aye, lad. Charles Ferrers is to marry Susannah. This voyage on which thou and I will venture life and limb is Susannah's dowry."

Chapter fourteen

Captain Tregarron was dour and strict, but he was a good seaman. *The Golden Way*, for all her bulk, went down the Channel at a fair rate. They made such good time that John reckoned they would sight the Madeira Islands before ten days were up. The wind freshened day by day and white clouds scudded through the sky, while the sea raced in long grey-blue rollers behind.

Soon the air grew warmer and men began to work th ship stripped to the waist. Matthew cast off his shirt and climbed the ratlines with the rest. And for three nights he groaned in his sleep, lying on his stomach to take the weight off red, blistered shoulders.

Strong and quick, and with John to advise him, he proved a handy sailor. Ben Churler, the boatswain, grinned at him.

"Art a paragon, Morten? To read thy book so sweetly and dance in the shrouds so nimbly. Hast no sin in thee?"

Matthew smiled cautiously, but said nothing.

"We shall see, 'ere we be done. Is that not so, Harry?"

And the bosun's brother answered:

"Aye, that it be, Ben."

The two of them grinned at one another. Matthew eyed them uneasily, but went his way. Days passed and the sun grew stronger; his skin healed and turned brown. Cape Funchal on Madeira fell astern. By and by the lookout spotted the great peak of Tenerife in the Canaries, like a cloud on the horizon. Tregarron looked grimly pleased and all hands went about the ship cheerfully. But Matthew knew he was being watched. He tried to avoid trouble by working smartly, moving quickly and, when work was not to hand, keeping out of the way.

He found himself a place in the shadow of the pinnace lashed to the foredeck, where he could shelter from the sun and yet escape the thick atmosphere of the forecastle and keep his eye on what went on. One afternoon he squatted there, his eye fixed drowsily on the Bible text he was to read that evening.

A shadow fell over the page and he looked up to see the smiling face of Harry Churler, the bosun's brother, looking down on him. Churler placed his sandalled foot quietly on Matthew's foot and pressed down. The pain was sudden and sharp. Matthew's body, tucked in beneath the small boat, had little room to move. He could not pull back his foot, yet would not, to save his life even, give Churler a sign that he could barely stand the pain.

"Why, Matthew, lad," bellowed Churler merrily. "So busy at thy Bible. Hast forgotten all else?"

"What do you mean?" gasped Matthew, shifting his position slightly and pressing down with his free hand.

Churler raised his voice again.

"Why, Matthew, lad, hast forgotten, so soon? Thou and I were bid go unlash the bonnet from the mizzen mast. The other sails are unbonneted already. Only ours is still to make. And here thou sits like a Christian with thy Bible and poor Harry works on his own."

Matthew freed his foot with a violent effort, rolled over and leapt to his feet.

"Thou liest in thy teeth, Churler. Lay off. Go do thy own task thyself."

"Why, thou art a Bible-eating whelp," whispered Churler amiably. He gripped Matthew's hair and jerked his head down below his waist. "Why, art a Bible-drinking, Bible-sleeping whelp," he added gently.

Tears of rage, pain and frustration filled Matthew's eyes. But he kept his head clear. Allowing his arms to drop, he let go the Bible and placed both hands flat on the deck. With a sudden jerk, he stood on his hands and let his heels fly over his head to land full in the face of the bending Churler. The hands loosened their grip on Matthew's hair. He fell to the deck and rolled over.

Churler, his nose bloody, staggered back and regained balance. Still grinning, as the blood trickled down on either side of his lips, he drew his knife and bore down on Matthew. The blade gleamed in a descending arc, and without thinking Matthew snatched up the Bible and held it before his face. The knife in its vicious swing drove right through the thick pages, the point bursting the leather binding. The Bible torn from Matthew's grasp dropped to the deck and lay there, the haft of the knife standing out from it.

In that instant, Tregarron came on them: Matthew struggling to rise from his knees, Churler staring open mouthed at the pierced Bible.

"Go forrard, Morten. Let the book lay."

As Matthew went forward, he heard Tregarron say:

"Churler. Thou knowest the penalty for drawing a blade on thy ship-fellow?"

"Aye, sir."

"And thou knowest the penalty for blasphemy?"

Churler hesitated.

"Aye, sir."

"We will inflict the second penalty. Go to the mainmast."

John Galton met Matthew in the forecastle and was told what had happened.

"And dost thou know the penalty for blasphemy?"

"Nay."

"I'll tell thee, lad. Churler will stand until sundown with a marline-spike thrust between his teeth and tied behind his head until the blood run from his mouth."

"Why, 'tis horrible."

"Aye, lad. The wrath of the righteous is more fearful than that of the wicked. But thou'rt not punished?"

"Nay."

"Would to God thou had been. For now Ben and Harry Churler have double reason to hate thee. Guard thyself. They are vengeful men."

But neither that evening nor the next day did the Churler brothers appear to take notice of Matthew. Their malice found another target – Satan.

As the ship ploughed on southward towards Africa, the black man spent his idle time perched dangerously half out along the bowsprit, head resting on folded arms, gazing out over the heaving waves. There he would stay by the hour and there he hung one day, when Ben Churler, the bosun, called him. Whether Satan heard the call or not, no one knew, but as he slid back to the deck there was a quick scuffle. No man saw what happened but several heard Ben Churler chuckle: "Why, blackamoor. Twenty lashes for thee, or I'm not Ben Churler."

Tregarron summoned the crew to the main deck. Satan, stripped to the waist, was strapped to a culverin. His body hung over the gun barrel like a meat carcass.

The lash began to fall and Matthew closed his eyes. But he could not shut out the awful sound as the blows landed. It was as though the keen leather cut into his own backbone and Matthew writhed at the thought. When the sound ceased and the men were dismissed, he opened his eyes briefly. The sight of the rounded back, with its bloodied, criss-cross pattern of marks sent him rushing to the ship side, where he hung over the water till his stomach came to rest.

"Will they not cut him loose and see to his hurts?" he asked John.

"Nay, lad, he'll stay there till sundown."

"But 'tis cruel, 'tis unjust."

" 'Tis ship life, lad. And look thou smartly, else will

94

Churler have thee athwart that culverin barrel and the lash at work on thy tender back."

Evening drew on and the black body still hung there in its coat of blood. Flies had settled in clouds. Matthew could no longer bear it. He went back into the forecastle and sought out Satan's sleeping place. Among the black man's few possessions he found what he wanted, a small pot of palm oil.

With this he went boldly down to the main deck, knelt by the half-conscious Satan and set to work. First he drove off the flies and cleansed the wounds. Then he carefully smeared palm oil over each stripe until the whole back was treated. When he finished, he saw Satan's eyes were open, regarding him silently.

A hand gripped his shirt neck, jerking him upright.

Ben Churler spoke.

"Thou has committed a fault, young Morten. Art not perfect, after all. And faults, among worthy men, must be punished. Dost know . . ."

A cry from the lookout cut across his words.

"Land Ho!"

Chapter fifteen

The setting sun on the starboard side cast a strange glow on the coast towards which the ship now sailed. From every corner of the ship men hurried to larboard, leaned over the side, or hung from the rigging to get a sight of Africa – land of dreams, wild tales and wealth untold. Not half a league away the surf boiled white on a shadowy shore; behind loomed a forest of giant trees and thick undergrowth, so thick that it looked like a black wall. And beyond rose mountains whose tops glittered in the sun's last rays.

"Shall we see yonder hills tomorrow and climb on them?" asked a young sailor.

Galton smiled. "Art homesick for Dartmoor, Dickon? Nay, lad. 'Twould be hard marching for a score of days to reach the foot of those mountains, through forest so thick thou must cut thy path, over marshes that swallow men whole, those that the beasts do not tear and the mosquitoes do not drive mad."

" 'Tis a cruel place. How do men live here, then?"

"Why, the rivers do carry their life, as thy veins thy blood."

"But, John," asked another seaman, "how shall we come by the blackamoors?"

"We'll not go to them. They'll come to us."

Sharp orders from the captain, taken up in Churler's cheerful roar, now sent the crew flying to their tasks. The ship turned to land, and drawn on only by her foresail, crept

96

in to shore. But while still a gunshot away, the captain gave orders to anchor. Then he had a small cask of wine broached and each man had a mugful.

" 'Tis no great shakes," said one, "but 'tis better than sour beer."

"Aye," said his mate, "my guts have grumbled with that cursed brew since we passed Rame Head."

"If we could go ashore," said another, "haply the folks there do brew strong drink."

"And haply with toads and adders therein to turn thee green."

" 'Tis not in question, for he be green already."

And so, in good humour, the crew went to their evening meal.

"The skipper's wise not to take us in through the breakers in this light," ventured Matthew.

John nodded. "Tregarron knows a thing or two. 'Tis healthier out here."

"John. Thou didst say the slaves would come to us. Was that a jest?"

"Nay, lad. The trade in flesh is strange and has its do's and do nots. A step from where we lie, by the river mouth, is a spot called Taresco. No town, but two stone houses for the traders. Beyond the shore, up-river in the forest, lie the towns of many peoples, each with their own tongue, strange ways and manner of worship. When they do quarrel, which, like men of our complexion, they do often enough, they do kill or capture their foe. Some captives they do eat, so I'm told, some they do make their servants. But since the Portuguesers found this place, captives are traded for knives, glass beads and pewter whistles. We shall lie here and wait to see what trade we can do."

"But what if the price be too high?"

John smiled. " 'Twill not. In Taresco be no more than a dozen men. They will trade on our terms."

"By force?" asked Matthew.

"By force and by agreement," said John, then laughed outright at Matthew's puzzled face.

"See, Matthew. This slave trade, with the Pope's blessing, is split between Spain and Portugal. So our visit here is a secret, between us and the traders here. But if it do come to the ear of the King of Portugal, then his man will report that the English did sail in with culverins a-thunder and blades a-flashing, and robbed him of his blackamoors."

"Why, 'tis deceit, twice over!"

John grinned. " 'Tis trade. And now, lad, time for evening prayers. Go seek in thy book for a text to square all. I'll go walk about the deck. 'Twould be Churler's way to leave poor Satan bound to the gun-barrel. I'll make sure he's cut loose."

At dawn next day the captain ordered out both boats and bid a dozen men arm themselves. Three men in each boat were issued with new arquebuses Abraham Combe had brought from Germany. Fitted with wheel lock for striking sparks, they had no need of the long slow match which easily became useless from damp. Tregarron picked older, steadier men to handle the guns, but promised each a hide-warming if they were not protected from the spray.

He put Ben Churler in charge of the second boat and took John, Matthew and Satan in his. The two boats raced for the surf line, but under John's skilled hand, their boat drew ahead and soon reached the southern bank of the estuary where two dirty white cottages and a ramshackle landing stage marked the Portuguese trading post.

Round the settlement hung a haze of heat and a stench of rotting vegetation. The man who came out from the first house looked much the worse for wear from the climate. His doublet and hose were shabby and stained, his collar open at the neck and his red-veined face streamed with sweat.

He introduced himself as Rodriguez and came straight to the point.

"Your fleet has left you behind, sir," he said.

"Our fleet?" asked Tregarron suspiciously.

"You are of John 'Awkins's fleet, are you not?"

"Nay, we sail on our own venture."

"I fear we have little to trade. Later in the year they will bring more ivory down-river. But just now is the wrong time."

"Any time will do for the trade we seek," said Tregarron brusquely.

"Aha," said Rodriguez. "Black ivory. There, I fear we have nought to offer. 'Awkins has, how shall I say, swept the board clear."

At first Tregarron seemed inclined to disbelieve him, but Rodriguez added quickly. "Captain, why should I deceive you, how would that profit me? No, Captain 'Awkins was not to be refused. A score of vessels, a thousand men — an armada."

Tregarron smiled thinly. "I will believe you, sir, even when you see double."

He turned to go.

"A moment, Captain. Do but try to the south, to Cap Roxo or Bissau . . .

"And, Captain . . . our wine stock is running low."

Tregarron waved a hand to Matthew, who went back to the boat and brought up a small cask of wine. The trader's eyes gleamed. "Try to the south, good sirs."

For ten days, *The Golden Way* sailed slowly to the south, putting in at river mouths, coast towns, forts. Many places were in better shape than Taresco, well fortified and with cannon which would salute the ship politely. The landing-parties would be met with some ceremony and the men invited to take part in entertainment. But Tregarron sternly forbade it.

And at every landing point the story was the same. Hawkins had been before them, sometimes only two days, and scoured the place. And Hawkins had changed his tactics.

He was no longer content to trade with the Portuguese, but went slave-hunting himself. A trader told Tregarron: "Your Mr Hawkins is too cunning to attack a town with his own forces. He seeks out a town under siege and offers his generous help, with men and arms, to the attackers."

At Conga, a day's march away, Hawkins's men had joined an attack, losing many dead, struck by poisoned arrows. Hawkins had only saved his own life by treating his wound with garlic. But they had set the town in flames and captured many slaves.

Tregarron held a council. His keen ear had detected grumbles from the men. They were tired of disembarking, rowing, returning to the ship, hoisting sail, lowering sail, and never being allowed into the townships.

"We can take but two courses," he told the crew. "We may land here, or farther south, and wait till our chance comes to profit from some local battle. Or we can sail far to the south, where even Hawkins has never been, and take our chance there."

Ben Churler spoke. "If we land and wait, we'll rot for sure, Captain. Men will take sick, and 'ere long the crew will not be fit to sail home."

Other men nodded.

"But," said Tregarron, "if we venture south into unknown lands, we set ourselves at risk."

"Better risk than rot," muttered a seaman.

"Thou hast never done either," retorted another.

The captain raised a hand to stop the argument, then Satan rose from the back of the crowd on the maindeck and pushed his way forward. Pointing south with his great arm, he raised his bent head and repeated:

"Coromantee. Coromantee."

"What signifieth that, man?" said Tregarron.

"Coromantee. South-west." Satan breathed. "Many, many black."

"I've known of this port, though have I never sailed there," said John Galton. "They do say the people there are fierce."

"Then will they make good purchase," said a sailor.

"If they do not boil and eat thee," came the answer.

Ben Churler stood up.

"I say we go watchful. The black heathen be cunning and we may be led into a snare. Be that not so, Harry?"

"Aye, that it be, Ben," said his brother. "What if yon Satan seeks to lure us to his own land, and there take sweet leave of us?"

"So he lead us there, he may go to the Devil hereafter."

"That he may not."

"Why so?"

"Why, 'tis the Devil himself. Look at him."

"Let be," barked Tregarron. "I say we sail where the blackamoor do lead us. Those who are for this course, bide still. Those who are not, let them stand aside." No man stirred. Tregarron nodded. "Now, on your feet, men. And do you, young Morten, sing for us the forty-sixth psalm."

Next day Tregarron had the ship stand out to sea, but set a course to keep the land in sight on the larboard side. While the ship slid along the coast, he kept the men busy. He tightened the reins of discipline. He punished men for coming late to prayers and even for more trivial offences.

The heat grew unbearable. Matthew found his own moods grow more sullen. One day when a badly handled line burned his hand he opened his mouth to curse. Galton clapped a hand over his mouth.

"Blaspheme not, O man of God. Curse not that ye be not cursed," he grinned. Matthew glared, then grinned back.

On the fourteenth day, Satan perched above the fore-topsail yard, gave a great cry and pointed to the land.

"Coromantee. Coromantee."

Chapter sixteen

The Golden Way now entered a huge bay, fringed with giant trees whose roots plunged into the water. Into the bay, from the heart of the forest, flowed a river, and on either side lay the streets and buildings of a bustling town. As the ship appeared round the horn of the bay, the people swarmed down to the beach. It seemed to Matthew that there were thousands. Out in the bay the din of their shouting and rushing to and fro sounded to him like the swarming of a multitude of bees.

"What if they be hostile?" he whispered to John Galton.

"Fear not, lad. We have given them no offence, as yet."

The water of the bay boiled into sudden commotion as dozens of canoes pushed off from the shore. The rhythmic splash and slap of the paddles punctuated the strange wild singing that urged them on.

" 'Tis a fearful sight."

"They mean to show their might. We must answer in like kind."

As if Tregarron had read Galton's mind, two culverins were run out, charged with blank. As the canoe flotilla came nearer, they were fired one after another, with a deafening crash and a fat cloud of smoke. On shore the forest responded with the shrieks of birds and monkeys. But the crowd on the shore were silenced. The canoes halted.

Her masts almost bare of canvas, the ship idled towards the river mouth, looming larger over the massed canoes as she drew nearer. One by one they pulled to the side and formed rank in two lines, leaving a clear stretch of water to the edge of the sand. Matthew gasped in amazement. For on the beach the crowd had split into two parts, leaving a way clear to the edge of the trees.

At the head of this great passage were massed more people, their clothes as bright as birds' plumage, in blues, greens, oranges and reds. Even from this distance, Matthew could see one figure stand out from all the rest, beneath a great awning held aloft by men around him.

"Aye, 'tis a great town and a mighty king," said John.

Tregarron appeared behind them.

"Galton. Thou art skilled in the Portuguese tongue?"

"I have some words."

"Then thou shalt be my spokesman. For I doubt the heathen prince will understand our tongue."

A boat party was made ready, with six arquebusiers, and all men armed to the teeth. "Let each man take with him two cutlasses, knives as well. Aye, and let there be two pikemen to go before me. And see that every man be cleanly dressed," said Tregarron.

He looked grimly at Matthew.

"Young Morten. Thou shalt stay on board. Thy charge is the blackamoor. They do say he hath been in the pearl fisheries of Margarita and swims like a fish. He shall not escape us now, though I doubt not that he intends to run away. When we know if there are slaves to be had in this port, the blackamoor may go to the devil in his own way. But until then, guard him well."

There was no great trouble for Matthew, for while the captain's party landed, Satan hung motionless in the rigging, staring at the shore, which Matthew knew must be his own land. He stayed there as morning wore on.

Canoes now began to circle the ship and the crew crowded to the sides to return the curious stares. Each canoe had some twenty on board, deep-chested men with huge heads, broad noses and gleaming teeth.

"They do seem a merry sort," said one sailor.

Harry Churler leered. "Why, they smile because they see thy chops and think how juicily thou'd grace their cooking pot."

It was past noon when Tregarron returned, his party in high spirits. Each man carried gifts of rich cloth and food. "And we did give them but the small coins from our pockets, and they were well pleased," said Ben Churler. "Were that not amiable, Harry?"

"Aye, that it were, Ben."

Tregarron's pleasure showed only in a faint smile. He called all hands together.

"Tonight we shall sup with King Orongo. Churler, let the men draw lots. Six shall stay on board and stand by the guns. If there be treachery, I shall fire my pistol and the ship party shall bombard the town. Make the most of your liberty, for tomorrow we shall start our business in earnest."

Lots were drawn, and Matthew found himself in the shore party. He went to Tregarron.

"Sir, what of my charge to guard Satan?"

Tregarron eyed him.

"Art a careful fellow, Morten. The king has given me word that he awaits the arrival, 'ere nightfall tomorrow, of a train of captives from the lands that lie beyond this forest. He has promised ten score men, women and children in return for the pick of our cargo."

Next morning, after the feast, Matthew, John, Boatswain Churler and two of the crew who were in a state to move, helped the ship-party ferry their drunken, semi-conscious crew mates back to the ship. Tregarron, face cold with distaste, had water pumped up.

Each woeful reveller was stripped and doused until he could stagger about the deck. Then the captain set them to clear the great hold beneath the maindeck. Some cargo was set aside to be taken on shore for the chief and his court to inspect. Matthew sorted out some 200 knives, 300 hatchets, some hundredweights of copper and lead circlets for use as armbands, and lead in the form of ingots. The cost of the whole cargo, he calculated, came to less than thirty pounds, less than one of the full-grown slaves would fetch if they could be brought safely over the ocean to New Spain.

If all went well, the voyage would make Abraham Combe rich enough to rival the Hawkins family and their friends. And it would enrich the Ferrers family, in more ways than one. As this thought struck Matthew, he bit his lip and tried to turn his mind to other things. But it galled him. No matter how he worked, for each pound he earned his rival Charles Ferrers would earn fifty. Unless Charles Ferrers did not return from his father's expedition. To his shame Matthew found he was calculating the chances of Ferrers being killed in battle.

He climbed back on deck. The ship was moving. Confident of his mission, Tregarron was shifting anchorage. While his crew made the hold ready for the new cargo, Tregarron had examined the water front and had discovered a steeply shelving reach where he might move the ship in close enough to let down the ramp and march the slaves straight from the land into the depths of the ship.

"Tregarron's crafty," said John Galton. "He'll have the slaves believe that they are imprisoned by the shore. Then he will take the ship out to sea before they know they'll never see their homeland again, and thus they'll not grieve."

"Why should he care whether they grieve or no?" asked Matthew.

"Tregarron cares not for their grief. But he'll not risk that they do themselves mischief in their grief. When we're at sea, they'll be too sick to care."

As the ship drifted towards the chosen spot, Matthew looked for Satan. He had not seen the black man for a whole day. But there was no sign.

"'Tis the last we shall see of Satan, I trow," said John. "Art sorry to see him go, Matthew?"

"Aye, though I rejoice that he has won safely to his homeland. I pray that he may find his own folk again, after his years away from them."

The ship now secure, the ramp went down with a crash. Churler posted armed guards at its foot to hold back the curious crowds who gathered round, amazed at the way the ship had opened up. Tregarron called up Matthew.

"Morten. You shall go down with me and oversee the accounting of the slaves when they bring them to the shore. Let Galton and two others be on hand to help."

Warriors from the chief's house now appeared by the waterfront and began to clear a wide space. All around, the crowds grinned and stared, shouted to one another, pointed to the white men and exchanged jokes.

" 'Tis like fair on a saint's day, Matthew," said John.

Now the excitement increased, people turning their heads towards the chief's house. The crowd made way for more warriors.

"Here they come. Here do come our good fortune," grinned Ben Churler.

First came two ranks of guards, long spears held sideways to make the way clear. Behind them, Matthew could see more people, moving slowly along.

John caught Matthew's arm.

"See. Our friend Satan did not go far."

Matthew saw Satan, his broad shoulders, bent head, his sea-man's garb marking him out amid the crowd. Satan raised his eyes to look where the slaves were approaching with their guards. John's fingers dug suddenly into Matthew's arms.

"He weeps, poor soul. Look how he weeps."

Satan's head had fallen again and his two hands were raised and pressed to either side of his face. The massive shoulders rocked to and fro.

"Thy prayer is answered, Matthew, but not in the way thou wished," said John.

"Satan has found his own people again."

Chapter seventeen

The ranks of guards passed between Matthew and Satan and hid the black sailor from his sight. Now came the captives, walking, or rather stumbling, in double file. Each went with his legs tied together at the ankles and each pair of men were yoked together by two forked sticks which fitted them like a collar and joined them rigidly to one another. No man could move faster, nor slower, much less try to escape, without strangling his fellow. Matthew counted thirty such pairs, mainly younger men.

Behind them, more loosely roped together, walked older men, their faces gaunt, their feet dragging in the dirt. Behind them came the women, old and young together, some bearing their babes in arms, some leading children by the hand. Even the children were linked together, like dogs on a leash. In silence they shuffled to a halt amid the crowd with its laughing faces and pointing fingers. Some dropped to their knees but at a jerk on their rope, writhed to their feet again.

The chief's men approached Tregarron, their arms wide to indicate the size of the slave column.

"Nay," said Tregarron. "We shall account for ourselves."

To Matthew he said: "Number them, Morten. Do it twice over and again when we have shackled them to take them on board. I have the king's word for ten score, and ten score I shall have."

"Can we not bid them sit down, sir? They seem half-dead with weariness."

"Nay, let them stand, that the count may be more strict."

"May they sit down when we have done?"

"Aye. But look to thy task, lad."

Matthew hastened with the count – but was too hasty. The numbers did not tally. Only on the third count, with John Galton's help, was Tregarron satisfied that the chief had not sold him short.

"Males in their prime, nine and forty, females in their prime, four and fifty, some in child; males and females past their prime, two and forty, male children, six and twenty, female children, eight and twenty."

Tregarron was still dissatisfied and argued with the chief's men.

"I did not think to have so many old ones, past their prime," he grumbled. "If they cannot be replaced with better flesh, I will leave them here."

"Nay, sir, 'twould be unwise," said John Galton.

"How so?"

"If we take away their ancients, the younger ones may sicken with melancholy and die. Besides, there are a round dozen of the women who will give birth 'ere long, and when that time comes, they will need the old women."

Tregarron shrugged. "So be it. Now, Morten, bring hither the blacksmith and let all be shackled."

"Not the women and young ones, for pity's sake, sir."

Tregarron glared. "Nay. There is not chain enough for that. But bid the blacksmith come and let us be away. I'll have them on board 'ere nightfall."

As the yoked branches were removed from their necks and the ropes cut, the men began to stretch and breathe deeply, but when the blacksmith and his striker began roughly to chain them, a low moan began to arise from the slaves. The crowd from the town began to drift away, and a cool wind off the sea made a rustling in the bushes.

"In the name of charity, haste and be done," barked Tregarron. Churler took up the words and began to curse the blacksmith, who bungled his work, drawing cries of pain from the slaves. As each pair of men were shackled they were hurried up the ramp and into the dark hold. Inside, other seamen clipped the ankle chains to bolts in the side of the ship. Churler bustled to and fro, chuckling and bidding his mates, "Lay them in close together. 'Twould be a sin if any should be left behind."

Some of the women and children, exhausted and afraid, would not budge from the ground. The crew seized them by arms, legs or hair and forced them to rise.

"Come, young Morten, be not idle. Thou knowest how the Evil One works among the idle. Give a hand, help our guests aboard," called Churler merrily. Reluctantly Matthew began to push and shove with the rest, making the unwilling slaves stumble to their feet. One of the children, a ten-year-old boy, suddenly bit Matthew's hand and made a dash for freedom. Without thinking in his pain and rage, Matthew cuffed the boy over his black close-curled head and knocked him to the ground.

"Handily done, Morten," called Churler.

Now the guards brought spear points into play and the rest of the slaves like unwilling cattle were raised up and driven into the ship. Two of the crew, bearing a great cauldron full of a steaming mess of beans and meal, followed them in and with a grinding roar, the ramp was winched up and made fast.

It was fast growing dark, but Tregarron did not hesitate. He had the foresail hoisted and, as soon as the wind turned, used the land breeze to take the ship slowly out into the bay. When he judged the distance from the shore to be enough to prevent any escape, he had the anchor dropped and told the crew they might go ashore. But he added tersely: "Any man that be not back by crack of dawn, has leave to stay."

That evening Matthew, uneasily pacing the deck, saw a

dark shape in the rigging, forward. He called the watch, who looked alarmed. "A blackamoor has escaped," he cried.

"Nay," said Matthew. " 'Tis Satan."

The black sailor pushed past them and ran lightly forward. Leaving the watch, Matthew followed him, but by the time he reached the main-deck, Satan had vanished. Look as he might, Matthew could find him nowhere. He went forward to his place in the forecastle and lay down in the close, thick darkness. At first, sleep would not come. One by one the crew came on board from the shore, some drunk, some quarrelsome, all excited. As each group settled down, they would cry to the next arrivals, "Peace, hold your cursed noise." But at length, long past midnight, all was quiet again. Matthew slept heavily.

At dawn, Tregarron paced the deck, irritably bidding the men go quietly about their work of getting the ship under way. But after the night's revels there was more than one thick head aboard, and here and there came the sound of curses and the crash of falling blocks, then the thud of blows as Ben Churler went his merry way amid the laggards. As the ship cleared the bay there was the first unmistakable sound of restless movement from below decks. Slowly rose a low muttering moan that swelled as the ship moved out into open sea and met the first rollers with a pitch and heave.

The sound rose higher and altered to a sobbing whine, a sound that was no word, but such as animals make when they are wounded. As it grew in strength, the two hundred voices in the hold seemed to strike one note, an unearthly wail that silenced the shouting and cursing on deck. Men stopped what they were doing and looked at one another in awe and fear.

The grin faded from Churler's face as the mainsail, half hoisted, began to slide down. The ship pitched more violently and lost way. Captain Tregarron appeared on the poop.

"In the name of God, get to work. I'll have the hide off any man that holds back."

As the crew moved uneasily into action again, Tregarron called:

"Morten, close the maindeck hatches more firmly. 'Twill keep down the noise."

"But, sir," protested Matthew. "They must have air. They'll stifle below."

"Do as I say and quickly, Morten."

Matthew leapt down on to the maindeck and bent over the hatch covers which had been propped open a few inches to ventilate the sweltering hold. As he bent to his task, he suddenly recalled how he had bent over the hatches of the ship in Plymouth Sound that night and bid the Flemish captives come up and take their freedom.

From the narrow gap beneath the hatch cover came a sudden hot blast of foul air, making him retch. He fell on his knees on the deck, then bent at the waist in agony.

"At thy prayers again?" shouted a passing sailor.

Matthew struggled up and went aft. John Galton was at the helm and took in at a glance his white face and staring eyes.

"Ah, Matthew, lad. Thy lady Susannah hath a sweet dowry, hath she not?"

Chapter eighteen

For two days and nights the ship ploughed westwards, blown by a lively wind that whipped off the wave tops and flung spray like fine rain across the ship. On the third day, as the wind began to lose force, Tregarron had the hatches opened and ordered men below to take water and food to the slaves and make a count.

The men came back on deck, green in the face and gasping from the foul air, and reported that six of the slaves, four old people and two children, had died. The captain ordered them below again to bring up the bodies, but this time they refused to go. The captain looked grim and Churler blustered, but no man would go down. In the end Tregarron was forced to let the men draw lots with a promise of wine for the two who drew a short stick.

The six bodies were dragged up through the hatchway and tossed into the sea to the sharks which had followed the ship since it had cleared the African coast. As the familiar wailing cry rose from below decks, hatches were hastily banged down, more sail was set, and the ship moved westwards again.

For several days Matthew kept to himself and spoke to no one. His voice was heard only at evening prayers, which he read in a flat dispirited voice. Tregarron looked grim, but let the matter be. But next day, on deck, John Galton confronted Matthew.

" 'Tis I who have offended thee, Matthew. Speak, is't so?"

Matthew dodged to one side, but Galton blocked his way. "Art angered by my talk of Susannah's dowry?"

" 'Twas a foul jest."

Galton's eyebrows rose.

"No jest, on my oath. I did mean what I said. Susannah's dowry, thy fortune and mine, too, sweats and rots beneath our feet."

Galton went on: "I know not what be worse for these poor knaves – to perish from the spears of their own kind, to die in our hands and be cast to the fish, or to die beneath the Spaniard's whip. Still, lad, come what may, we must sail on. We have boarded this ship and must sail her to the bitter end."

Another five days' fair wind, another 200 leagues and the ship fell becalmed. Old hands watched the glaring sky and sun which appeared to hang over the maintop gallant and speculated how long the calm would last – two days, four days, a week? None could say.

By this time another eight slaves had died, including a young man, and Tregarron now began to look anxious. He had the hatches flung wide open, and the whole ship filled with the reek of sickness and suffering. Around the ship the oil-smooth water was cut by the fins of prowling sharks. The crew, too, began to lose appetite and sicken. The captain had the hatches closed again and said that they should be opened each day for two hours only.

He drove the crew about their work, but there was little enough to do. The sails hung limp. Off watch the men began, at first secretly and then more openly, to dice and play cards. Churler waited to see what Tregarron would do, but the gloomy captain seemed not to notice. Matthew grew tired of searching his Bible for the rousing and encouraging verses that Tregarron demanded of him. "Find verses that do not speak of death, sickness and the like . . . let us have nought of Job and such . . . let us have cheerful verses."

Amid his gear, Matthew found again the tiny book which

Susannah had given him and turned the pages listlessly. But now the poet's pleasure or pain in his love seemed foolish and trivial.

A week passed in the calm and now the death toll rose to twenty. Three of the women had given birth, but no one could say if the babies would live or not. In place of dicing, the men now began a gruesome game, wagering first the coins in their pockets, then money they had not earned, on the number that might die next day. Everywhere was gloom, muttering and sometimes open grumbling.

Alone Satan prowled the ship, peering and prying into corners, moving off when approached, head down, leg trailing.

"The blackamoor plots some evil," murmured Ben Churler. "I'll swear he rises when we sleep and doth open the main hatches. We shall keep our wits about us, or he'll let loose his fellows and cut all our throats. Be that not so, Harry?"

"Aye, that it be, Ben," replied his brother. And the two of them took to watching Satan more closely.

Two nights later they discovered the black sailor kneeling by the open hatch. They swore he was about to climb down into the hold. Tregarron seized his chance to make an example.

Next day he paraded the crew in the stifling heat and had Satan tied to the mainmast in full view. No number of lashes was ordered. Tregarron bid Churler, "Lay on 'till I say 'Hold'."

The lash rose and fell. Matthew counted ten, a score, two score. His head felt dizzy, his knees began to bend. He tried to shut eyes and ears, but the sound of the lash went on.

"Hold," cried the captain. Satan hung by his wrists at the base of the mainmast. The crew dispersed, each seeking a place in the shade. The ship fell quiet, and in the silence came the buzz of flies seeking the blood on Satan's back. At the sound, Matthew stirred himself and walked to the forecastle. The men busy with cards did not see him search Satan's gear and take out the palm oil. He went back on deck. Tregarron was back in his cabin, the Churler brothers nowhere in sight.

Slowly, averting his eyes from the sight of Satan's back, Matthew approached and knelt down silently beside him. The touch of his hand aroused the black man. The heavy head slowly turned, the eyes, rolling white, silently regarded him. Then Satan spat full in Matthew's face.

At sunset, Satan was set free. To the astonishment of the crew, who could not remember such a lashing, he rose to his feet without help and went forward with slow, slithering step. One of the crew watched him go.

"Now shall we all look to our throats," he muttered, "but Ben Churler most of all."

After evening prayers, Matthew went forward, climbed up to the beak deck and sat down, back against the bowsprit base. The shock he had received had passed, and he began to ponder soberly why the black man's hate had sought him – who had wished Satan no harm. Then, in a flash, he recalled the day when the slaves were loaded. Satan had stood in the crowd and watched him – Matthew – number his own people like cattle, shove them, force them to rise, even beating their children. His heart grew sick at the thought, but sicker still to think that all this had gone by and he had given it no thought until tonight.

To calm his mind, he took out his little book of poems. It opened at a familiar page.

"The stars be hid that head me to this pain
   Drowned is reason that should be my comfort
   But I remain dispairing of the port."

He turned back the pages to the front of the book.

"Matthew Morten, his book," and underneath, "From his friend, Susannah Combe."

He stood up in the darkness, listening to the lap of waves below the bow. Then with an angry swing of his arm, he threw the book far out into the sea. It disappeared with the faintest of splashes.

Swinging down from the beak deck, he made his way aft, purposefully and swiftly. Over the foredeck his feet thudded, down the steps on to the main-deck. Down on his knees by the hatches. He jerked back the bolts and with a surge of strength heaved up the hatch covers one after another, oblivious to the sudden gust of foul air from below. Something moved on his left, which he saw only with the tail of his eye. He straightened up and looked into the face of Ben Churler, beaming with satisfaction.

"Oh, a great fault, Master Morten. A great sin, beyond remission or redemption."

Matthew eyed him with contempt. Still smiling, Churler advanced round the open hatch. And stopped. And stiffened. And raised both hands to his throat. Churler's body, pushed down by an unseen force, bent backwards. Over the lowered body loomed the silent face of Satan. The black man's hand rose slowly. Something flashed.

"In the name of God, do not," cried Matthew, in sudden terror.

His cry echoed through the ship and brought men running with lights.

But the knife in Satan's hand sliced down and Churler's body slid to the deck.

Daybreak brought a sudden breeze, and Tregarron had the crew hoist sail. The wind freshened and soon the ship was moving at six knots. The captain kept the men on the move. But they worked unwillingly, their faces on the body of Ben Churler, sewn into a shroud, which lay by a gun port.

Half-way through the morning the wind dropped again. Tregarron cast his eye up at the heat-hazed sky and then called the crew to the maindeck. He wasted little time, but looking coldly at the triple rank of sweating men, he said:

"Ben Churler, our bosun, is dead. Harry Churler, his brother, shall take his place. Churler!"

Beaming, Harry Churler stepped forward.

"Aye, Captain Tregarron, sir. You may . . ."

Tregarron cut him short. His eye now fell on Matthew.

"Morten. We have a matter to regulate that concerns thee. Thou'rt young, rash and a fool, but a godly lad. For what thou did last night, six lashes shall be thy portion. And 'ere we turn to graver business, you shall receive your punishment. Six lashes, and Galton shall lay them on."

Matthew looked at John Galton, but the helmsman looked away. "To the gun," ordered Tregarron. But Matthew walked there of his own accord, stripped his shirt and leaned his chest across the gun metal, now scorching hot in the sun.

"Lay on, Galton," called the captain. "If thou do not justice to thy task, there'll be three lashes for thee for each one for Morten."

As Galton came near him, Matthew said out of the corner of his mouth:

"Lay on, John. I'd not have thee suffer hurt."

"Quiet, lad. I can lay these lashes so there's more noise than hurt. Better I do it than one who hates thee."

"Why, spoken like a true friend."

"Hm, thou hast begun to learn wisdom with age."

The lash fell, and with each blow it seemed to Matthew that some part of his past life dropped away like the book falling into the sea the night before, with his dreams and hopes.

He forced himself to rise and picked up his shirt. Controlling the weakness in his legs, he strode back across the deck and fell in with the rest of the crew.

"Each thing in its season," said Tregarron. "Next, caps off, and Morten shall say a prayer for our shipmate, Ben Churler." He gestured to Matthew as though to bid him make haste, and Matthew was glad to comply.

"Now," said Tregarron to Harry Churler, "bring forth the blackamoor."

Satan, arms strapped to his side, was led on deck. Tregarron turned again to the crew.

"There be younger men here who perchance know not the penalty for murder at sea. We can ill spare to lose a hand, but justice shall be done. A man that hath murdered his shipmate shall be tied to the body of his victim and cast with him into the sea."

"Nay," gasped Matthew.

"Aye," replied Tregarron. "See to it, Churler, and make haste."

While Satan twisted and strained, three men took hold of Ben Churler's shrouded body and lashed the black man to it. They hefted their double burden to the ship's rail and with a quick heave hurled it into the sea. Impulsively Matthew broke rank and rushed to look down, but there was nothing to see but the hurrying ripples of sharks' fins.

"Aloft, all of ye," roared Tregarron. "The wind doth come. Will ye stay here and rot?"

The crew raced up ratlines and along yards and heaved on the dried, cracking canvas. But there was no wind. The ship stayed still. The sun now straight above the mainmast burned down and the crew peered into the greenish depths of the sea and muttered: "Think on it. Churler and Satan down there, bound like brothers."

"Did I not say Ben Churler should watch his throat?"

" 'Twas a fearful penalty."

" 'Twas a fearful crime."

"This voyage will bring us no good. I feel it in me. There's others will never see Plymouth again, I trow."

When evening prayers were done, men not on watch huddled in the forecastle. They talked uneasily of past, unlucky voyages. One hand, older than the rest, began to tell how the ghosts of men killed at sea would walk on the water and follow the ship for miles, and even try to climb on board and haunt their shipmates. But John Galton bid him hold his mouth, and all fell silent.

Matthew slept, but his sleep was full of horrific dreams. He woke suddenly. All was dark on deck, save for the ship's lanterns. It must be just after midnight. He rose and slipped out of the forecastle. Within yards he stumbled over the sleeping figure of the starboard watch, but he let the man lie. Something drew him on, down to the maindeck.

As he clambered down the steps, he knew what was wrong. His nose caught a whiff of the stench from the holds. The hatch must be open. But who had done it? Who would dare? He stopped, heart bounding, his belly gripped by the familiar feeling of ice and fire, his eyes fixed on the darkness beyond the open hatch.

Rising from the deck was a figure that seemed to glitter green with seawater. Silently it edged around the hatch, dark and menacing.

Matthew gave a strangled cry. The weird figure silently whirled and leapt upon him, in a reek of sweat and the stagnant sea-water.

"Satan!" gasped Matthew.

Chapter nineteen

"Satan!"

As the muscular hand seized his throat, Matthew knew in a fleeting instant that this was no ghost, but a flesh and blood Satan, saved by some chance from the sharks.

In that instant too, Satan knew him, and loosened his hold. The two crouched down beside the hatches.

"Satan. How can you be alive?" whispered Matthew. The faint light of a smile gleamed in the black man's eyes.

"Rope," said Satan. He breathed deeply, swelled the muscles on his chest and arms, then suddenly breathed out, letting the muscles shrink. Matthew understood. By stretching his body as it was bound to Ben Churler's corpse and then letting the muscles go slack, he had made space inside his bonds. And as the sea closed over the two of them, he had writhed clear. It seemed unbelievable. But Satan had served the pearl fishers of Margarita. It would be no great effort to swim below water. All that day while the ship lay becalmed, Satan must have clung to the timbers of the ship, unseen by the crew.

"But, Satan. The sharks?"

"No blood. No sharks."

"The crew will slay thee."

Satan nodded.

"Hide. No find."

"Hide? Where?"

Satan pointed downwards and Matthew laughed at himself for a fool. Among the slaves in the darkened hold, where only the unwilling food-party went each day, Satan might lie hidden till the voyage was over. But then?

"How shalt thou escape when we come to port?"

Satan's eyes gleamed. He pointed to his own chest.

"Not run away."

He pointed down to the hold again.

"All run away."

Matthew stared. "Nay, 'tis folly."

Satan's head rose. "My people, father, sister. I go. All go."

"But how?"

The black man did not answer, but beckoned. Matthew, bewildered, found himself following Satan down the vertical steps into the hold. At first he held his breath; then his lungs heaved and his chest filled. He choked with the stench. He had thought himself used to the foul air, sickness and filth, but here it was ten times worse. Yet men and women and children still clung to life here, though two score had been flung to the sharks.

He could hear them all around him as his foot found the bilge-soaked planks of the hold. They breathed, snored, moaned in their sleep around him. Here and there a child whimpered and its mother took it to her breast. Here and there a boy or girl cried out, a sick person gasped. They were all round him, but he could see nothing. Satan grasped his arm and pulled him down the centre of the hold. Here on long shelves lay the young men, their ankle-chains rattling as they turned in their sleep. Some little way in front of them a light gleamed.

"Satan," whispered Matthew. Satan's grip tightened. His voice hissed in Matthew's ear.

"Name, not Satan. Name Ba-umba."

The light, a rope-end dipped in oil, flickered and smoked but faintly lit a small space amidships. In the circle of light sat an old man. His sunken eyes were open as though he never slept. Across his legs, resting her head on his thin thighs, a girl slept. Ba-umba now moved into the light-circle and knelt down by the girl. The old man's face twitched. He put out a thin hand and carefully ran it over Ba-umba's head. A painful smile creased the old face into a hundred wrinkles and tears spilled over and ran down his cheeks like rain on parched ground.

The old man spoke softly. Around them people stirred, chains clinked, voices muttered. The chattering spread, and amid the noise the name "Ba-umba" was repeated. A high-pitched command from the old man made all quiet again and in the silence Matthew noticed that the girl was awake, staring at him, curious and afraid. Ba-umba drew him forward and indicated by hand pressure that he should bend down. The old man's hands touched the top of his head and traced the line of his jaws, the nose and lips, a light dry touch, like a bird's claw. Matthew forced back an impulse to flinch away. Now Ba-umba was speaking with his father. He sensed the others were listening, tensely.

Ba-umba squeezed his arm.

"Matt-ew. Help. Cut irons?"

Matthew thought a moment. The silence deepened.

" 'Tis folly, Ba-umba. But I'll help. Tomorrow, I'll hide files in the meal cauldron. But 'tis folly. Young men can run away, but the old and children will never get clear of port."

"Not port, Matt-ew. Island. You tell captain. Island. Slaves walk, eat, get fat. Good price."

Matthew nodded. The idea was crazy – eight score people old and young, sick, babes in arms, to escape. But could it be worse than what awaited them?

"I will help," he told Ba-umba.

Again Ba-umba spoke to his father. Again the buzz of voices quickly silenced. The girl reached out and touched Matthew with her finger.

Matthew now climbed back from the hold alone. The deck was empty, though lit by moonlight. He carefully replaced the hatch covers. No one, it seemed, had noticed.

It was still only a little time after midnight. Barely an hour had passed since Satan, who was now Ba-umba, had risen from the sea.

But for Matthew, a great age had gone.

Next morning, when the crew drew lots for the party to go down into the slave hold, Matthew seized the chance to take the place of one of the two men chosen. This was easy enough, for none viewed the task with anything but loathing. He removed two iron files from the cargo, wrapped them in sailcloth and, when his companion was not looking, slipped the bundle into the cauldron of steaming beans and meal which was the slaves' daily food.

Down below they handed over the cauldron to the women and checked the number of the slaves. Two more had died. They must have lain dying in the night as he stood among them. The dead were an old woman and a child, pitiful bodies, scrawny legs and swollen stomachs.

"Why dost linger, Morten? God's name, lad, let's away. Take the legs, I'll take the arms," his mate muttered. Matthew followed him reluctantly, peering round in the half-darkness. But he could see nothing of Ba-umba.

On deck, all was bustle. Clouds massed on the horizon. A wind was rising, starting its song in the rigging. The calm was over. As the sails strained with the wind, down came the rain. With cries of joy, the crew, half naked, capered round the decks and raced in the ratlines, holding back their heads to drink in the water, rubbing it into their skins as it streamed down back and chest. Only the dour Tregarron was unmoved, and sternly ordered the barrels to be set out on deck and a spare sail rigged to act as funnel to catch the rainwater. Now *The Golden Way* headed for the west again. By nightfall the rain had eased up and great jagged gaps opened in the clouds through which the stars shone. But the wind blew steadily.

Going quietly below, Matthew raided the stores again. He set aside a dozen files, knives and hatchets, wrapped them in sailcloth and hid them. Then he went to Tregarron and, looking the captain straight in the eye, reported that he had made a false count and certain stores were missing. Tregarron nodded.

"So be it, Morten. Do thou but mark it up against thy share when the voyage ends."

"Gladly, sir," said Matthew impulsively.

"Jest not, Morten. It becomes thee ill."

"Nay, sir, 'twas not in jest. The stores are my charge, and 'tis my fault if the count be false. But, sir, how long 'ere we make landfall?"

Tregarron rubbed his chin and, beckoning Churler and Galton, put his head together with theirs and calculated. "By my reckoning another ten days' sailing will bring us to Dominica and five days beyond that to our first port of call on Terra Firma, the mainland of New Spain."

"Sir, I have thought over our cargo, how we may best ensure that we have good profit therefrom."

"How so?"

"Sir, we have lost two and forty out of our two hundred. One hundred, eight and fifty remain, of whom, to my reckoning, two and thirty are sick and may die."

"Nay," said Harry Churler, "that cannot be."

"Give me leave to differ, Bosun," replied Matthew. "I did go below today and made careful count. 'Tis as I say."

"And, art a doctor?" sneered Churler.

"Nay, but 'tis wiser to fear worse than to hope better and be balked of one's hopes," said Matthew.

Tregarron broke in impatiently. "What has thou in mind, Morten?"

"I would, sir, that we should find an island where no man lives, 'twixt Dominica and Terra Firma. I have read there are many such. There we may bide a few days, make repairs to the ship, take in fresh water and game. The slaves, well guarded, we may walk on the beach and see they be well fed. A fat slave is worth more than a thin."

"I like it not. What if they do run away?" said Churler.

"Why," said Galton, with a swift glance at Matthew, "we be four and twenty, well armed. We are men, not children, and can look to them well. I say Morten speaks sense."

"I fear some mischief," said Churler.

"Have done with your quibbling," said the captain. "Morten has a sound head on his shoulders. 'Twill cost us nought and reward us well. Galton, knowest thou of such an island?"

"Aye," replied John. "There be plenty not more than twenty leagues from Cartagena – a good port for our sale."

Tregarron nodded. "Good, then let us make all speed to Dominica."

Delighted with the success of his ruse, Matthew now waited for a chance to go below again. This was not easy. He could not twice take another's place on the food-party. But each day he managed to slip a package into the meal cauldron.

Two days west of Dominica he decided he could wait no longer. He seized his chance on night watch and slipped below to speak to Ba-umba. He learned that half the fetters were filed through. The rest would be cut by the time the ship was off Cartagena.

By the time the ship reached the uninhabited island, the slaves would be ready.

"But how if this be discovered, when the ship be drawn to land?" asked Matthew.

Ba-umba had his answer ready.

"Before land, captain speak God. You make long prayer. We run."

The boldness of the plan was desperate. But what other chance was there?

"Fear not, Ba-umba. I'll do my part," said Matthew.

He climbed back on deck and silently dropped the hatch

cover into position. Then his heart gave a great leap as he felt his shoulder seized. He tried to turn round but could barely move in the powerful grip of the man behind him.

John Galton spoke.

"In God's name, have a care, Matthew. 'Tis a dangerous game you play, and I fear Harry Churler is wise to thee."

Chapter twenty

On the fifth day west of Dominica, Tregarron changed course to the south-west. Two days more and a small smudge, like smoke, appeared on the skyline, to a shout of "Land" from the foremast top. By noon, the island John Galton had spoken of was in full view, its forests vivid green against the blue of sea and sky. As the ship under reduced sail drew slowly nearer, the richness of the vegetation, the great girth of the trees, and the yellow gleam of the sand made a young sailor say: "Why, 'tis the Garden of Eden."

"Ah, but where be Eve?" mocked his mates.

"So I get my feet on that shore and can go hunt game in those woods, can Eve shift for herself," he replied amid a shout of laughter.

"Shift thyself, then, Dickon," grinned Churler, "or thou'lt be chosen ship-watch, while thy mates run merrily after groundhog and hare."

"Doth this land have hares, then?" asked the lad, wide-eyed.

"Aye. With seven legs, three arms, no less. And they can wield both sword and pike, so guard thyself, Dickon, lad."

Now the shore-line opened to show an inlet guarded by a long sand bar. Tregarron had a man swing the sounding lead and fathom the way in from the bows. But all went smoothly.

"Hast chosen well, Galton," he told the helmsman. "This isle has all the look of a privateer's hide-out. There's more ships than this one have been careened on this beach, I dare swear."

Galton said nothing, but putting the helm over, brought the ship round to slide into a natural channel that ran through to within yards of the nearest trees.

"She can ground here, like she were in dry dock," he told Tregarron. "Shall I take her in?"

"Aye, Galton, take her in as far as she'll go, but let her not heel, else will the ramp not fall freely down. I've no mind to bring the blackamoors up two by two through the hatches."

As John Galton took the ship close in to the shelving bank, Tregarron told Churler bid the men get ready to go ashore.

"But first, let every man spruce himself and we shall give thanks to God for a safe passage."

"Shall I read the lesson, it being morning prayers, after a fashion?" asked Churler. Matthew, who stood nearby, caught his breath.

"Nay," said Tregarron. "In charity's name, not this time. Art a godly man, Churler," he added drily, "but hast a voice like a crow. Let Morten do't. Come hither, Morten. Hast a good verse to restore our spirits?"

"Aye, that I have – the 104th," responded Matthew.

"Then, go get thy Bible. And, Churler, have the men gather on the main-deck."

As Matthew went forward in search of his Bible, he felt the ship shudder and come to rest. The masts rocked and blocks rattled, the hull lifted a fraction, but as Galton had promised, the lie of the land and water held the vessel as though in the palm of a hand and the deck stayed level. Faintly below he heard the movement of the slaves. They must know now that the ship had come to rest. His task was to give them time for their attempt to escape the ship. The rest was in their hands.

He picked up his Bible from his gear and stood a moment

studying the pages he had chosen. Nearby an old sailor rooted among his belongings.

"Matthew, lad. Hast a good text?"

"Aye, Thomas, I have. Art glad to see land?"

The old man turned a weary eye on him.

"There be but one land I would see and 'tis old England. Pray we may have a quick run, a good sale of our cargo, a fair shareout and a good sou'wester all the way to Rame Head."

"That I will and right gladly," responded Matthew quickly, and as quickly thought to himself: I am a good hypocrite already. What I now do will rob this old fellow of his share and all his mates. We shall one and all lose all we hoped for.

The captain's voice cut short his gloomy thoughts.

"Morten. Step lively with the Book."

Matthew ran aft. The crew had gathered on the main-deck. As he came down, he heard the captain say to John Galton:

"While we do make our service, thou and one other shall break out arms from the casks and get down to yonder bank."

"There's nought to fear on this isle, but groundhogs and parakeets," said Galton.

"I fear nought for what may come aboard," returned the captain. "It is that which may leave the ship I have in mind. Go to't and, Morten, read thou the lesson."

Matthew took up the Book and faced the crew, who now stood in ranks before the mainmast, the captain and Churler a little to one side. On shore, in the shadow of the ship, stood Galton, and another sailor, arquebus at the ready. From the shore came a background noise of birds in the forest, like Plymouth Cross on Market Day, thought Matthew wryly.

He began to read: "Bless the Lord, O my soul . . ."

Beneath his feet came a scuffling sound. Some of the crew muttered uneasily, but Tregarron's glance silenced them.

"Who laid the foundations of the earth that it should not be removed for ever . . ."

As the psalm unfolded, Matthew felt his muscles relax. Without effort he pitched his voice higher, almost singing the words.

"So is this great and wide sea, wherein are things creeping innumerable . . . There go the ships . . .

"Thou hidest thy face, they are troubled: thou takest away their breath, they die and return to their dust . . . Thou sendest forth thy spirit, they are created . . ."

The psalm drew to a close. The hold beneath his feet was silent now, a silence that was uncanny and disturbed the crew more than the noise had worried them before. But still nothing happened. As he read the last verse, without drawing breath, Matthew went on to the next psalm. He saw a quick frown move over Tregarron's face, as if some doubt had struck him, but Matthew raised his voice still further.

"O give thanks unto the Lord, call upon his name . . . Remember his marvellous works that he hath done . . ."

Now, he thought, I must hold them. He lowered his voice and changed his tone to that a of storyteller, telling the tale of the Israelites as they wandered from land to land, of their time in Egypt.

"He sent a man before them, even Joseph, who was sold as a servant, whose feet they hurt with fetters, he was laid in iron."

The meaning of the words he was reading unprepared suddenly struck home to him. Did anyone else notice? The noon air was hot, sweat began to trickle down his face. Men raised an arm here and there to brush away buzzing flies. The captain looked steadily ahead. Churler's face was bland, baby-like in its round, red cheerfulness. Matthew looked down and caught John Galton's eye.

"The king sent and loosed him, even the ruler of the people and let him go . . ."

From below decks came a steady rumbling, a rising sound

as if the slaves tramped their feet. Matthew spoke more loudly, telling of the plagues sent to trouble the Egyptians.

"And did eat up all the herbs of their land and devoured the fruit of their ground."

Now the slaves were singing, a deep-throated chant. Below him, Galton and his fellow-guard shifted their weapons from hand to hand. On deck the crew fidgeted. Matthew raised his voice still further, till he was shouting above the unearthly sound that swelled up from the hold.

"He opened the rock and the waters gushed out. They ran in the dry places like a river . . ."

Now it seemed the ship was shaking with the tramping, chanting sound.

"And he brought forth his people with joy and his chosen with gladness."

With a great rending crash, the ramp burst open and fell upon the bank. John Galton and the other seaman were thrown to one side like sacks of chaff. As the crew broke ranks and rushed to the ship's side, the slaves, in a black, jostling throng, poured out down the ramp, stumbled on to the sand, dragging themselves up, mothers swinging children up on their backs, young men half-carrying, half-pulling old men and women.

"God help us," cried a sailor. "D'ye see who leads them on? 'Tis Satan. 'Tis a spirit risen from the dead."

"Quiet, thou fool," rasped Tregarron. "To arms, men, and to the beach. We must stop them 'ere they get deep into the forest where we may not find them."

There was a moment's confusion before the men swarmed down ropes and leapt on to the soft sand. Matthew was with the first and raced to where John Galton lay motionless, half in and half out of the water. Grasping him by the shirt, Matthew dragged him on to the sand. Galton's eyes opened.

"Nay, Matthew. Was too well done," he gasped painfully. "Thy friends have slain me."

A thin streak of blood appeared at the side of Galton's mouth. His chest jerked.

"Nay, 'tis not true, John," cried Matthew in tears. "I'll get help and bring thee back aboard. Thou'rt barely hurt."

"My hurts are inward, lad. Nay, I'm going, where pray God I'll find little Mary and the rest once more. But hark, Matthew . . ." his voice died to a choking whisper. "Matthew, get thee into the forest . . . or Churler will take his revenge on thee."

John's head fell to one side, the eyes stared up at the sky. Matthew looked round. Half the crew were gathered on the shore, with Tregarron among them. The other half must be already in the forest, with Churler leading them.

Matthew clambered to his feet, picked up his cutlass and ran for the trees. The captain called his name, but he neither answered nor turned round. In a moment he was among the bushes and running hard. Where he was heading he could not say, but he knew he must put distance between him and the rest of the crew.

He stumbled over a root and fell on his knees. When he rose again, his clothes were sodden. The ground away from the beach seemed to grow more waterlogged. As the trees closed in above him, he lost sight of the sun, and before he had run two hundred yards, he had lost sense of direction altogether. From his left came the murmur of voices. He turned sharp right and ran on. The undergrowth thinned out, but the ground grew more muddy. The way sloped down. He must be heading for a river. Would that bring him back to the shore? He turned left again hoping he was heading upstream. His breath came harder now and his pace slowed down.

Ahead something flashed white. Barely fifty yards away was a group of men, Churler among them.

"Young Matthew . . . we do need a word with thee . . ."

The amiable voice reached him faintly, but already he had turned aside. Which way? There was only one, back towards the river. He hesitated and saw Churler raise his arm. He rushed to the right, slipped and fell. His clothes were mired. He threw away his cutlass and struggled on, bent double, now on firm ground, now up to his knees in slime. Through the trees he saw water, twenty yards away. Could he but reach and cross the river . . .

Tripping, stumbling and sliding, he made the last twenty yards and fell into the water. It struck cold on his sweating, mud-stained face.

"Matthew!"

Churler's voice seemed to come from only a dozen yards away. Matthew waded out into the water and made ready to launch into mid-stream. In that moment he heard the click of a crossbow being wound. He dived. Too late. There came the twanging snap of the bolt.

A tremendous blow pitched him down into the water and the light vanished from his eyes.

Chapter twenty-one

Matthew opened his eyes. Above him were palm leaves, green and ribbed, but motionless and packed close together. A face appeared above him, old and wrinkled. Black eyes peered down into his. A strong hand raised up the back of his neck and a gourd was placed to his lips. Liquid flowed into his mouth. He swallowed and fell back.

"You sleep five days."

Matthew opened his eyes again. Above him were palm leaves, but now he could see that they were laced together to form a roof. From somewhere a sweet cool breeze blew over his face. He pushed out an arm. He lay on a bed of what seemed to be leaves, but he was covered with some kind of sacking. He was alone. But near him he could hear the sound of voices, children playing. The ground outside the hut was bright with sunshine. He pushed back the sacking and tried to sit up, but felt dizzy and lay back.

The old face with its dark eyes appeared again. An old woman was at his side, grinning. She offered him a broad leaf like a platter, on which juicy meat steamed. Now he felt hungry and ate greedily. The old woman gave him a drink from a nut shell and he fell back to sleep again.

When next he woke, Ba-umba sat by his side. The eyes beneath the massive scar gleamed.

"Now, you sleep ten days."

Matthew stared at him, head whirling. Ba-umba — Satan — the ship . . .

"Did all escape?"

Ba-umba laughed deep in his chest.

"All run away. Hide by river. Tre-garron men run all ways. We stay. They go ship. Angry. Men fight. Ship go."

"But, I . . ."

"You wounded – in water – we see." Ba-umba rose. "Come."

Matthew got up from the bed, to find that he was naked. Ba-umba threw him a piece of rough cloth.

"My shirt, breeches?"

"Gone." Ba-umba showed him how to tie the cloth around his waist. "Come."

They went outside. Matthew stared. They stood in the main street of a little town of some twenty huts, all built in the same way – a palm-leaf thatch hung on a cross beam between two forked branches. At one end of the village was a larger house with a big open fireplace before it. To one side arms – cutlasses and pikes – were stacked. Ba-umba followed his gaze and laughed.

"Ship go – men angry – leave behind."

Under an awning, on a three-legged stool, sat the old chief, Ba-umba's father. Around him stood or squatted other old men and some women. All were dressed in loin cloths, though some had wound cloth round their heads. The children who played in the dirt of the clearing were quite naked.

As Ba-umba and Matthew approached, people followed them until, as they stopped in front of the old chief, a crowd had gathered. A young man brought forward a log and the chief bid Matthew sit down. He sat awkwardly, hitching the cloth round him, and the young girls in the crowd pointed and giggled. They murmured one word over and over.

"What do they say?"

"They call you white boy."

The old man now began to speak slowly, his remarks

interrupted many times with cries of agreement from the crowd. Ba-umba said:

"My father tell. You good."

Matthew shook his head.

"My father, Akanoro, say, you be one – with Talusi."

"What be Talusi?"

Ba-umba waved his arm at the people.

When the old man had finished speaking, women busied themselves at the fireplace. Then others spoke, seeming to Matthew to be repeating Akanoro's words. But no one seemed to tire and the speaking went on as the sun began to set. When the speaking was done, the sunlight had been replaced by flames from the fire. Over the flames, wild pig were roasting. The talking died slowly and slowly the eating began. Matthew tasted cautiously. There was pork, small game birds, something that might be rabbit, a fresh-baked bread, strange-tasting fruit, and sweet liquor from the nutshells.

Young men and women began to dance, first in advancing and retreating lines, then in circles, the girls twisting, the men leaping high, waving sticks. Older men played on whistles cut from long cane, or beat on log drums. Watching the dance, Matthew became aware that it was like the telling of a story in actions, the voyage, the suffering in the hold, the escape, and the final dance of victory.

The old man turned and spoke to Matthew. Ba-umba grinned.

"My father want – you sing."

Matthew stood up and the crowd grew silent. The flames died but the embers still glowed bright. He looked at the strange faces around him, and had a sudden clear picture of the congregation in church at home.

He wondered whether it were Sunday or not and realised that he knew nothing of what day it was. He knew only the time of day. He closed his eyes and opened them again. The mind-picture of the church at home was gone, and in front of him were the black faces, young and old, skin shiny glossy in the firelight. In the hush of the forest clearing he began to sing. When he reached the end of the hymn there was silence, for a moment.

"My father want – you sing again."

Matthew sang again, another hymn, and this time was conscious of voices in the background putting a strange harmony to the tune he sang. His voice responded until it seemed to him that he no longer sang his own tune, but something else. He stopped and sat down. Voices in the crowd went on singing, others picked up the harmony, and soon the clearing was full of song, a thrilling chant like the one he had heard that fateful last day aboard *The Golden Way*.

Next day he wandered round the village. In the "main street" he found young men awkwardly hefting pikes and cutlasses. One turned to him and thrust a cutlass into his hand, bidding him show how it was used. So for two hours, until the climbing sun made the exercise uncomfortable, he trained them in the use of the weapons. He spoke to them as John Galton spoke to him and marvelled at the way they seemed to understand. And as the young men fought, they called out and Matthew repeated their words. At first his voice made them stagger to and fro and roll on the ground with laughter. But soon they became accustomed to his voice, and their delight as Matthew called out commands in their language, knew no bounds.

Next day, when he rose, the young men awaited him, pikes and cutlasses at the ready. Those who had not pikes or cutlasses shaped themselves spears from branches to which heated and flattened knife blades had been fixed. In the use of these for both stabbing and throwing, Matthew had nothing to teach and much to learn. Some of the older men made bows and arrows, tipping the arrows with small stones ground to a sharp edge, or with sharpened bone, or by burning and polishing the wood to a point. These they taught Matthew to use, though he could never match their skill.

Days, weeks passed. Matthew tried to keep note of the passing of time, but found it difficult. He believed that the ship had come to the island in January 1568. So now it must be April. But there was little variation in season and so little to guide him. For several months he kept a long stick in which he cut a notch for each day. But in the end he stuck it in the ground outside his hut and left it. After he placed it there, the children avoided his doorway, but looked curiously at it from a distance. In the end he found himself watching for the waxing and waning of the moon and so kept count of the months.

After six of these months had passed, Ba-umba told him that a party of young men, with canoes they had shaped from logs, would journey to the mainland.

"Why?" said Matthew.

"To seek a better place for our home."

"But on Terra Firma the Spaniards have their homes. 'Tis perilous."

"True. On Terra Firma also are Cimaroons."

"Cimaroons?"

"Thus Spaniards call the slaves who run away and live in the forests. The Spaniards fear them. Cimaroons come at night from the forest, burn the Spaniards' houses, drive off their cattle – and kill."

Matthew nodded.

" 'Tis clear. You would join them."

Ba-umba smiled grimly. "Aye. But first, we find them."

So, for another six months, parties of young men, led by Ba-umba, combed the inlets and bays on the mainland, seeking traces of the Cimaroons. In time, Matthew went with them, learning to take his place and paddle with the rest. Sometimes at night they passed close by the white houses of Spanish settlements, and once they passed a large port whose lights shone out to sea. But at first they found no trace of the Cimaroons.

Then one day an escaped slave was found wandering in the forest near a Spanish plantation and the canoe-party brought him back to the island. His language was unknown to the Talusi, but he knew some words of Spanish. By slow questioning, Ba-umba and Matthew learned from him that not far away were two ports, one Nombre de Dios, which lay on one sea, the other Panama, which lay across a narrow neck of land on another sea. Between the ports ran a road, and in the forests north and south of that road were two Cimaroon towns. The one to the south, he said, was big and had a thousand men.

Ba-umba laughed and shook his head, but now gave orders for a new expedition, the largest so far, with six canoes carrying every young man that could be spared. Matthew asked if he might join them. Ba-umba smiled and said, "Aye. Who would sing if thou did not come?"

This time they made landfall in a natural harbour guarded by a string of islands lying a mile or two off. Above rose a steep hill from whose top the country road could be viewed for miles. They climbed the hill and Matthew saw the satisfaction with which Ba-umba studied the place. Far off along the coast could be faintly seen the roofs of a port, which Matthew thought must be Nombre de Dios. Ba-umba had the young men hide the canoes near the shore and the party made camp for the night in the forest.

Next day, the party, some forty young warriors, prepared to march. Ba-umba reckoned that the Cimaroon town, if it lay where the escaped slave had told him, must be six hours' march away.

At first the going was tough, the undergrowth thick and tangled, and they had to hack their way through. But later on higher ground they made better going and steadily made their way to the top of a small hill from which they might get their bearings.

But as they reached the crest of the hill, the leading marchers came running back to where Ba-umba and Matthew walked in the main column.

"Come," they cried. "Come."

Ba-umba and Matthew ran forward through the trees and burst out into the open.

Down in the forest, not three miles away from them, hung a thick, twisting pall of black smoke.

Chapter twenty-two

Ba-umba sent two warriors ahead down the forest slope towards the smoke column which now mounted high in the air. Then he led the main force more slowly through the woods, which grew thicker as the ground descended. As they marched, the Talusi dropped their lighthearted banter and were silent, loosening cutlass or knife, shifting grip on spear or pike haft. Matthew knew once more the familiar hot-cold sensation of fear and excitement.

The scouts suddenly reappeared through the bushes.

"Cimaroons dead. Town burnt," they gasped.

"The Spaniards?" said Ba-umba.

"Gone." The scout pointed towards the coast.

"Come," said Ba-umba, and set off at the run. The others followed, Matthew keeping close behind him, dodging trees, leaping over fallen logs and marshy ground, forcing a way through bushes. The air was warm with noon-day heat, but the sun did not break through the branches. They ran in a green haze, sweat running down faces and chests.

Now the trees thinned out. Matthew could see the shapes of huts, half destroyed and still smouldering. The burning smell grew stronger, more sickening. Then they were in the clearing, a huge one, for this had been a big town. Around them in a circle the ruins of twenty huts were falling apart, spreading their ashes.

Matthew stopped, horrified. The ground was heaped with black bodies, dead and dying, young and old, warriors still clutching spears, women with babies in their arms. There had been no battle, but a massacre. The attacking force had run amok, slaying those who resisted and those who could not.

But even in his horror he still noticed, curiously, that the dead were dressed in white man's fashion, women in long gowns, now ripped and bloodied, men in shirts and breeches. His eye caught a gleam of light. He knelt and saw that one woman wore a crucifix round her neck.

Ba-umba's men searched the village. But all that remained were the dead or nearly dead. He called over the scouts and gave them rapid orders. They set off down the trail that led away south-east towards the coast. Then Ba-umba bid the other men to lay out the bodies carefully in the shade of the trees. His eyes ran shrewdly over the clearing and he nodded several times. He turned to Matthew.

"Too bold. No heed for danger. They were attacked by surprise and paid the price."

Now the scouts were back. As the still hot ashes of the murdered village showed, the attacking column had not gone far. It was moving down the road to Nombre de Dios, slowly because of captives and the load of booty. Some of the soldiers were half drunk on palm wine.

"How many Spaniards?"

"Three score."

"How many captives?"

"Two score, young women and warriors."

"How do they march?"

"Thirty ahead, with ten on horseback, ten to the rear. The rest on the flanks."

Ba-umba nodded. He beckoned the warriors to him and they squatted around him while he cleared the ground and drew with a stick his plan of attack. It was simple and direct. He turned to Matthew.

"Will you fight with us?"

Matthew looked round at the devastated village.

"Willingly."

"It will be hard. We shall kill every one. No prisoners."

"I will fight with you."

"Good. Come."

The Spanish column moved at a leisurely pace, and noisily. The officers, tunics unbuttoned, shirts open to the waist, lolled on their horses and they slowly made their way home to Nombre de Dios. The foot soldiers, pikemen and arquebusiers straggled along, some stopping now and then to drink looted wine. The Cimaroon captives, half-naked, bruised and bleeding, roped two and two together, stumbled along at the rear, loosely guarded by soldiers who no longer bothered to keep station but laughed and chattered among themselves. Some of the rearguard, completely undisciplined, had dragged back several Cimaroon women and halted. A quarrel broke out, two men seizing a woman and each attempting to grab her for himself. The others gathered round, one officer trying to separate them, others egging them on with shouts of encouragement. It was here that Ba-umba struck his first blow.

Twenty Talusi, using only knives, matched man for man with the rearguard party, silently moved from the bushes at the height of the quarrel. Most of the Spaniards died without knowing whence the blow had come. A few shouted, or tried to draw sword. One fell on his knees and begged for life. All died, and ahead of them the rest of the Spanish column wended its noisy way. Two warriors ran ahead through the bushes to give their report to Ba-umba, who waited with twenty men some hundred yards beyond the Spanish advance party.

In front rode a heavily-built middle-aged man with a grey moustache, a Spanish veteran, and at his side a young man newly out from Spain. They chatted easily to one another. Both were well pleased – one that his career in New Spain should have such a fine ending, the other that his career should start so well.

"So much for the legend of the fierce Cimaroons," said the young officer lightly. The veteran frowned.

"Thou'rt mistaken. 'Twas no legend. This village had grown careless. They believed the legend too much."

"A pity, though. No more action for men at arms in this region."

"Mock not your future, young man. I shall be thankful if in two days' time I may board my ship and sail for Seville again. 'Tis ten years since I was home."

The young man laughed.

"Have no fear on that score. There's none to harm . . ."

The sentence ended in a shriek as a silent arrow from the bush cut off his speech for ever. The older man jerked his horse round and began to shout orders. But a second arrow cut them short and with it all his hopes of seeing Seville again. As he crashed from his horse, volleys of arrows flew into the panic-stricken mass of mounts and men. From either side in the bush rose the war-cry of the Talusi, and two waves of black warriors fell on the demoralised Spaniards.

Those officers who stayed on horseback in the mêlée were swiftly dragged down. Two struggled to their feet and, placing their backs to a tree, tried to defend themselves. The last they saw was two men, one black, broad and scarred, the other sunburnt and lean, leaping on them with savage blades.

Unable to clear space for pike-work, the foot soldiers struggled to draw their swords. But the fury of the onslaught overwhelmed them. Those at the rear, leaderless and terrified, tried to escape, only to run straight into the arms of their Cimaroon captives, now freed, re-armed and merciless.

Matthew fought in a haze of mad anger that blurred his vision. The weapons of his foes seemed to hold no fear for him. He did not feel the wounds he received. All that was real for him was his own fury and the sight of those mangled bodies lying amid the burnt-out huts. Only when the battle ended did he feel the pain of half a dozen cuts and see the blood flow down arms and legs. In a flash he remembered John Galton's words as they trained on the Hoe.

"Fight not like a gentleman, with hand on hip and pretty stance. But fight as the poor do, for very life."

Aye, John, he thought, as he looked round at the dead horses and men, the exultant faces of Talusi and Cimaroon, I have learnt thy lesson well.

He heard Ba-umba shouting. The Talusi were forming into column of march. They had lost three dead and a handful wounded, and these the Cimaroons were laying on stretchers made from Spanish pikes and officers' cloaks. Others gathered up the captured arms and fastened them in bundles. Then together the two groups marched back to the stricken village, to the mournful task of burying the dead.

With a cruel firmness Ba-umba would not allow the Cimaroons to stay. No sooner was the earth stamped down on the graves than he had the column on the march, Talusi paired with Cimaroon, and heading for the bay where the canoes were hidden.

That night they made camp on the hills above the sea, and a strong guard, made up of Talusi warriors, was posted. Ba-umba and Matthew sat together in the midst of the young warriors who talked of the battle that day, their eyes glittering and hands waving. Every now and then one would point at Matthew and there would be laughter.

Matthew tried to grasp the meaning of their rapid talk, but it escaped him. Ba-umba laughed.

"They say, thy name shall not be White Boy, but The Singer."

"Why so?"

"In the battle, thou didst sing songs to thy God."

Chapter twenty-three

Next day, on the camp-site, a small village was quickly built. Matthew marvelled how the Talusi and Cimaroons could work together, even when their languages were not the same, to build the neat strong huts. Ba-umba was amused.

" 'Tis but a shelter for the Cimaroons. Soon we shall build a true town, over there." He pointed to a spot where a stream flowed into the bay.

Matthew stared. "Will the Talusi live here?"

"Aye. Here we will make our stronghold and from here we will plague the Spaniards."

"Have you not plagued them enough?"

" 'Tis but a beginning." Ba-umba turned to speak with the leading warrior of the Cimaroons, who looked troubled. Ba-umba told Matthew: "Some will go back to their own village that was burnt, where they have lived many years. But others will not. They fear it is no longer safe."

"They are right. What hast thou said?"

"Nought. Yesterday I brought them away lest the Spaniard should pick up our trail. But now they must choose what they will do. We shall go back to the island and speak with Akanoro, my father."

The returning canoes, laden with Spanish weapons and clothes, were greeted with great joy by the Talusi village on the island. Matthew had seized the chance to fit himself out with shirt and breeches, and some of the young warriors had followed his example. At first the old men frowned, and some quietly returned to the loin cloth, but others continued to copy Matthew's way of dress.

When the Talusi council met, there was little opposition to Ba-umba's proposal that they should shift their home to the mainland. Matthew suspected that Ba-umba and Akanoro were already in agreement.

The old chief argued that they were far from the spirit of their own true home across the sea, that one resting ground was as good as another and that as soon as possible they should find a home where Talusi might "live and die". When the young folk heard Ba-umba describe the new home they demanded that the canoes be loaded at once.

But even when agreement was reached, the move was still delayed. The old men decided that the whole people should move together. This meant more canoes had to be built. Matthew hit on the idea of building a sailing boat and, aided by some of the young men, he set to work. But they had neither the proper tools nor experience. Ba-umba found the solution, recalling boats he had seen on his travels. Two canoes were fixed together with rough-hewn planks, and a mast stepped on the platform thus made between them. The elegant cloaks taken from the Spanish officers were sewn together and rigged as sails. The first trials proved successful and more were built. And so after a month, the Talusi set off for their new home. They had been on the island for a year and a half, Matthew reckoned, and their number, with births and deaths, was now one hundred and seventy.

When the Talusi landed in the bay Ba-umba had chosen, they found only a score of Cimaroons waiting, men and women. Their leader told Ba-umba that the rest had returned to their destroyed village to rebuild it. He could not say what had become of them.

"Will they betray us?" asked Matthew.

Ba-umba grinned.

"Oho, the Spaniard will find us soon enough. If we do not find him first."

The rest of that year (which Matthew thought was 1570) was spent in building the new town. First, stockaded strong-points were set up on the hill above the shore and on one of the off-shore islands. These were manned day and night by guards who carried horns made from shells found on the shore. The sound from these horns could be heard a full mile off.

Next the town was laid out with fine roomy houses, whose palm-leaf walls were extended almost to the ground to guard against chill breezes that blew off the sea at night. Matthew noticed that several huts had been built and left empty and asked Ba-umba about them. He pointed up the hill to where the remaining Cimaroons lived.

"Can we not bid them come down and be one with us?"

"Nay. Not yet. In time," replied Ba-umba.

Matthew, aided by his friends, built himself a small hut a little away from the main street. And just a little way off in the trees he built another hut. Here he would go, when he reckoned it was Sunday, and hold service, reciting psalms and prayers. Afraid of forgetting the texts now he no longer had his Bible, he had scratched his favourite passages with knife-point on large pieces of bark, stripped from the trees. Outside his "church" he set up a stone carved with the name "John Galton: died 1568". Around it he planted small flowers, and soon they grew and covered the head-stone. On Sundays before service he would take his knife and cut away the flowers and moss that clung to the stone, and clean out the outlines of the letters. But the flowers and moss always covered them again.

That summer came heavy rains and the houses near the

stream were flooded. The floodline was carefully marked and the houses rebuilt farther up the slope. When the rains died away the clear skies and hot sun returned. The forest trails began to dry out.

Ba-umba had the young men begin their war training again, and Matthew drilled some in the use of the captured arquebuses. But he told Ba-umba they were useless without powder and shot.

"Soon we shall have both in plenty," Ba-umba replied.

A war council was called, with the Cimaroon warriors coming down from their hill village to take part. Plans were sketched in the sand, past campaigns and battles of the Cimaroons against the Spaniards were gone over, forces were counted and their strength assessed. Then scouts were sent out, overland and along the coast, to bring back reports of Spanish garrisons at different points from Nombre de Dios to Tolu.

Now there were one hundred Talusi and Cimaroon warriors. But it was agreed that as yet they should not combine. Three fighting units were formed, one of Cimaroons, two of Talusi. A kind of working language in which words of both languages, as well as Spanish and English, were freely mixed, grew up between them. Ba-umba led the main Talusi force. A Cimaroon, who had the Spanish name of Pedro, led the second company, and the other Talusi band chose as their leader "The Singer".

On New Year's Day, 1571, by Matthew's reckoning, the three groups attacked. A Talusi force in canoes swept into Tolu, boarded four Spanish caracks and sent them down to the bottom of the harbour in flames. Three small settlements along the coast were overrun, and a fort on the outskirts of Nombre de Dios itself was taken by storm.

Next day the governor in his palace received the wild reports of bewildered survivors. The numbers of the attackers were wildly exaggerated, the reports altogether fanciful. The captain of one of the caracks in Tolu, indeed, declared:

"The Cimaroon who led the assault on my vessel was of a lighter hue than the rest, and did sing hymns in the English tongue."

The governor shook his head and wrote to the viceroy. He urged that the next mule train with gold and silver which should come overland to Nombre de Dios from Panama in the spring should be sent under double guard. The viceroy agreed and, for good measure, changed the date and route of the convoy. The ruse seemed to work and the mule train, laden with half a ton of ingots, reached almost to the gates of Nombre de Dios in safety. The attack came just as the guards had relaxed and were thinking of eating and drinking in comfort in the city. The mule train captain reported to the governor.

"The Cimaroons, señor, did drop from the trees like monkeys, crying 'Yo Peho'. Our men fled like dogs, such was their fear. Our mules and weapons the Cimaroons took away. But the gold, Excellency, they sent me to say, is hidden in a hundred different places in the forest. They said they took it only to vex us."

Now the governor begged the viceroy to ask for reinforcements from Spain. The viceroy noted the request and passed it on with his next dispatch by fast boat to the king in Madrid. He added in his own writing: "The Governor of Nombre de Dios has no stomach for his task."

That spring the Talusi and Cimaroons judged the Spaniards had no heart for a counter-attack. Big stretches of forest were cleared around the town and the first crops planted.

With the crop planting went big celebrations. Some of the Cimaroon men and women married Talusi people and moved down the hill into the main town. A number of them, who bore Spanish names, had been baptised, and they came, very shyly, to Matthew's hut on Sundays to hear his service. But he sternly made them remove their gold crucifixes before he would allow them inside his church. Some agreed, but others were angry and disputed with him.

Akanoro heard of this and was highly amused.

"Is your God not the same?" he asked Matthew.

"There is but one God," Matthew replied, "and in his Book it is written that there shall be no images in his house, for such is the way of the – heathen." He spoke the last word in English.

"Hea-then? What manner of men are they?" asked Akanoro.

Matthew, suddenly embarrassed, was silent.

Next Sunday he ignored the crucifixes and paid no attention when one of his congregation crossed himself. Matthew made up simple rhyming verses in a mixture of three languages to fit the hymn tunes. When they sang together the tunes became altered. He altered the pitch of his own voice to fit in with theirs. And when all sang together, the faces in front of him would fade and in their place would be the features of the poor Plymouth folk crowded at the back of the churches, lost in the enjoyment of words and music.

Crops were gathered. The rains came and went. News came of a Spanish expedition to destroy the "Cimaroon Fortress". The Cimaroons went by night to the plantations and passed on false rumours to the slaves there. In this way, when the Spanish troops set out, they were led in the wrong direction.

Lost in the forests south of Panama City, the Spanish force wandered for several days in hopeless confusion. Straggling back to Nombre de Dios, it was attacked each day by small forces of Talusi and Cimaroon warriors. It reached Nombre de Dios in a shattered state. When he tried to fix the date of these events, Matthew was no longer sure whether he were in 1571 or 1572. But he found that he had no need to know. It was enough, in talk, to say, "the time we came here", or "the time of the floods", or "the time of the mule train capture", and everyone understood.

With the spring were more marriages, absorbing the

Cimaroon village into Ba-umba's people. When the feasting time came round some of the Cimaroon Christians asked Matthew to preside over their marriages. Matthew asked Akanoro's permission, and when the old man agreed, Matthew prepared himself carefully. With the aid of a mirror found in a Spanish mule pack he cut his own hair and clipped the straggling beard that sprouted on his chin. He put on a new white shirt and black doublet, part of the booty from the same raid.

In a space cleared before Akanoro's house, he stood with the young couples in front of him and the whole town gathered round. While the sweat streamed down his face and soaked his clothes, he commanded them to join hands and declared them to be wed. From the boisterous crowd came cries of "Sing", "Sing". He sang to the new harmonies he had learnt. The people joined in and without a break the young men and women formed two lines and began to dance. They carried him with them and he danced, stripping off to the waist.

Amid the heat and excitement, he found himself facing Kulokela, Ba-umba's sister, the girl he had first seen, so long ago, in the faint tow-light in the depths of the slave hold of *The Golden Way*. They advanced towards one another and she smiled at him, her teeth gleaming.

Later that night he found himself at Ba-umba's side.

"Your sister has not married," he said. Ba-umba eyed him curiously, the eyes gleaming beneath the great scar.

"Kulokela has not made up her mind," he said.

Chapter twenty-four

One day came a report of a vessel lying off the coast some miles away towards Nombre de Dios. The Cimaroons said it was not Spanish, but might be an English or French privateer. It was light, rakish and heavily armed. Matthew's curiosity was aroused and, taking with him one or two companions, he searched the coastline carefully for many miles. After a month's careful work he found what he was looking for – a hideout and store.

It lay in a small bay concealed from all sides and sheltered from the winds. Neatly concealed in sand and undergrowth was a big store of food and equipment. To Matthew's growing excitement he noticed that the stores were familiar in appearance. He searched among the casks and bales until he found a ship's name. It was *The Swan of Plymouth*. The ship must be from his home town.

A week later a scout reported a ship off the coast again. And again Matthew hastily launched a sailing canoe and set off, this time alone, to the hideout. A column of black smoke met him. By the beach a great tree had been set on fire and the fire was dying out as he paddled in to shore. Nailed to the tree was a rough board and scratched on it a message – a warning. Matthew stared at it, bewildered for some moments, until he realised that it was in English.

It was a warning from a captain called Garrett to another called Francis Drake, that "the Spaniards" had discovered his store and he should take care. Drake – thought Matthew –

that name is known to me. He had seen him in church with John Hawkins – a dare-devil face with sandy moustache and beard. His father had been a prayer-reader like Jacob Morten, and there were a whole tribe of brothers, all seamen.

Matthew sailed back to the town and went with all speed to Ba-umba. "We must send and speak with this captain when he arrives. He will be an ally against the Spaniards."

"No." Ba-umba's reply was terse.

"Why should we not?" demanded Matthew angrily.

"Francis Drake. I know this man. He was with Lovell's fleet that brought black slaves to New Spain. His vessel brought me back to Plymouth."

Matthew nodded. All that he had forgotten. Ba-umba saw Matthew's face drop and put a great hand on his shoulder.

"Let us see, Matt-ew. Perchance this man Drake is here to harass the Spaniards. But perchance he is here to sell my people to them."

Matthew nodded. But he kept watch on the coast that summer. And in June he saw three ships appear and watched from a nearby hill while their crews landed. They wasted no time, but set to work to build a log stockade, five-sided, with two sides facing the sea and a gap through which boats could be drawn up. Matthew crept down to the edge of the tree line and hid where he could hear the men talking. Scraps of their conversation told him that two ships were from Plymouth, *The Pascha*, with Francis Drake in command, and *The Swan*, with his brother John Drake as captain. A third ship under a man called Rance had joined them only lately. Drake's men expected little of him and were sure he would soon leave them.

But best of all, Matthew learned that the ships carried no slaves and few goods for trade. They were here after Spanish silver and gold – but at as little cost as possible.

He rushed to report this to Ba-umba, but he still shook his head.

"If they see my people, they will want to sell them. It is easier than fighting for gold. Let us see them fight the Spaniard first."

A month later the ships left the bay. They were headed for Nombre de Dios.

"Good," said Ba-umba. "Matt-ew. We two shall go and see these men at work."

They launched a sailing canoe and sailed along the coast to a point some five miles short of the port. There they landed and, hiding the canoe, they circled the town and hid themselves in a wood near one of the forts. They made themselves comfortable in the branches of a large tree that gave a good view of streets and houses and settled down to wait. Towards night they slept in turn. Ba-umba woke Matthew when it was pitch black, for the moon was still down.

"Men marching," he whispered, pointing towards the harbour. As he spoke the bells in the town church began to peal. Drums beat, lights flashed. Men rushed with lighted slow-matches into the central square. Below men appeared, rushing the fort, and then on into the town. Now the battle raged round the market-place. It seemed the Devon men were attacking from both sides. Shots mingled with the clash of pike and sword. More shouting and the sounds of battle faded away. The English had driven the town forces out by the eastern gate and were scouring the streets with torches.

Ba-umba signalled to Matthew. They slid from the tree and headed for the harbour.

"Now, what sayest thou, Ba-umba? This man Drake does without a thought what we have never done. He has marched into Nombre de Dios in full battle order."

"Aye. He had ships with cannon at his back."

"And if we go in with him, so shall we."

Ba-umba nodded. "Let us go down to the shore and seek his rear party."

On the beach they could see no one, but Ba-umba's keen eye spotted pinnaces some way from the shore.

Matthew cupped his hands to his mouth.

"Are you Drake's men? Tell him the Cimaroons would talk with him."

The only answer was the splashing of oars.

"Cowards," spat Ba-umba. "They row away."

"Come back, friends," shouted Matthew. But the boats only drew off into the darkness.

Ba-umba laughed. "Drake took with him all his brave men. Come."

"Let us wait till daylight and sail over to Drake's ship," said Matthew. Ba-umba looked doubtful, but agreed. When light came, though, the sea was empty. Drake's little fleet had sailed away. But where?

Sadly Matthew steered the canoe back to the bay where Drake's ships had anchored. It was deserted. Yet Drake could not have sailed back home, not so soon. There must be another hideout among the tiny islands off the coast.

"We must wait," said Ba-umba.

For three months no more was seen of Drake, but there were reports of attacks on Spanish ships, of captures and sinkings, all of which brought a grim smile to Ba-umba's lips.

"I think we shall meet Drake soon," he said. He sent out canoe patrols each day, along the coast and, in September, one patrol caught up with John Drake and several men in a boat at the mouth of a river the Spaniards called Rio Diego. The two groups fixed a rendezvous a fortnight hence in that spot and each party went back to its base.

A day before the rendezvous, Ba-umba and Matthew led a strong detachment to the river mouth and set up a hut on an island in mid-stream. The whole area for miles around was searched to guard against surprise. Then, at dawn next day, Ba-umba and Matthew waited under an awning outside the hut, surrounded by a strong guard. Before long, round the angle of the river mouth, a ship hove in sight. Matthew recognised Drake's own ship, *The Pascha*. Pinnaces were lowered and rowed smartly towards the island. A dozen men, heavily armed, landed, Drake at their head. By his side Matthew recognised his brothers John and Joseph. And, as they approached, he waited for them to recognise him, but, if they did, they gave no sign.

Matthew translated Ba-umba's formal greeting and compliments on Drake's reputation and deeds against the Spaniards, but Drake gave him no more than a curious glance. Did they not even recognise his voice, or had that changed too?

Drake replied warmly to Ba-umba and said that the Cimaroon fame had spread far and wide and struck fear in the Spaniards' hearts.

"Our voices even struck fear into thy men, one night in Nombre de Dios," Ba-umba said ironically.

Drake smiled wryly.

"They were feared even of their own shadow. Why, I did tell them afterwards that I had led them to the treasure house of the world and did they seek to run away from that?"

"Yet, you found no treasure."

"Nay, there was silver in the governor's house, but the gold had not come overland from Panama."

"'Tis true, but next month the gold fleet will arrive there. Then, if you will, we may make sport with the Spaniards."

"With all my heart," said Drake.

Ba-umba signalled to his men, who brought up tables and stools and bade Drake and his men sit down and eat. There was roast pig, baked fish, dried beef, cassava bread made from the roots of yucca, poultry, coconut juice and palm wine to drink, and the English sailors ate with relish.

"If we had known that it was gold you sought, we could have given you plenty," said Ba-umba idly.

Drake stared: "Could have given?"

"We robbed the Spaniards of it and hid it in the woods, beneath a stream. But the stream is now in flood and we cannot come near it."

Drake's face fell.

"Why bury the gold?"

"We buried the gold to vex the Spaniards. For ourselves we do not need it. For what shall we use it? Iron we can use for weapons and tools. But gold is too soft to make a cutting edge. We fight the Spaniards for revenge."

Drake nodded. "So be it. We fight them for gold. But let us fight them together."

"Agreed," said Ba-umba. "When the plate ships tie up in Panama Harbour, we shall send you word. But tell us where we shall find you."

"If you have nought against, my men shall fortify this island. Our main force has business elsewhere. We'll return 'ere four weeks have passed."

As the meal ended, John Drake leaned forward and asked Matthew:

"Tell us, 'Maroon Boy, whence did thou learn thy English?"

Ba-umba laughed. " 'Maroon Boy is as English as you."

The Drake brothers and their companions looked astonished. "Well can I now see that his hue and features are different from thine," said Drake to Ba-umba. He turned to Matthew. "Who art thou, young man, and where from?"

"Thou hast heard my voice in Plymouth church 'ere now," replied Matthew.

"How so?" they asked, astonished.

"My name is Matthew Morten, son of Jacob Morten."

"Why, 'tis not possible. 'Tis known in Plymouth that Matthew Morten died four long years since, when he sailed in these waters in Abraham Combe's ship, *The Golden Way*."

"So men say I am dead?"

"Aye, and others that 'tis well so."

"What means that?" demanded Matthew.

" 'Tis what some men say. *The Golden Way* never came home to Plymouth. She was sunk by a Spanish ship and but seven of her crew came home — Harry Churler and some others. He put it round the town that Matthew Morten helped their slave cargo to run from the ship and thus did beggar them all."

Matthew nodded. " 'Tis true. I did help the slaves to run from the ship. This chief to whom you speak and his people are they."

Francis Drake spoke.

"Aye, one man's misfortune turns to another's advantage. Let us have no more of that tale. We are now comrades in arms. We care not what is said in Plymouth taverns."

"Have you news of my family?" asked Matthew eagerly.

Drake's face darkened.

"Bad news, I fear, Morten, lad. Brace thyself. Thy mother is dead. These past two years. She went to Exeter to nurse her own kin in the plague and came not back. 'Twas a sweet woman in word and deed."

Matthew bent his head. Ba-umba, who had guessed the meaning of the words, gripped his arm. Matthew swallowed and bit his lip to check the tears.

"Nay, lad," said Drake, "weep if thou wilt. 'Tis no shame."

The others looked away a moment.

"And my father?" asked Matthew.

Drake hesitated.

"He's well and hearty," he said carefully. "What news else is there, lads?" he went on.

One of his men grinned wickedly.

"John Hawkins and his kinsman Francis Drake went a-visiting to San Juan de Ulua, and had to kick their way out again through the Spanish plate fleet."

The Drake brothers laughed.

"Aye, England and Spain be no longer such sweet friends."

"A new church be built at St Budeaux."

"Plymouth hath a new Guildhall . . ."

"Aye, and a new grammar school . . ."

"There be new wharves on South Side, by Sutton Pool."

Matthew asked, "How doth Abraham Combe, my old master, and Sir Henry Ferrers, his partner?"

The Drake brothers exchanged glances.

"Why, both are dead."

"Dead?"

"Aye. Sir Henry died of a fever in Malta, on his last campaign. His son is now Sir Charles, though that signifieth precious little, for the estate's not worth a groat. Abraham Combe – aye – well might thou ask, Matthew Morten . . ."

"What means that?" asked Matthew.

"Why, Combe did lose all in that slaving venture. When thou let go the slaves, then did all Combe's advantage slip through his fingers. More than that. He had borrowed from men in Exeter, expecting a rich return. And lost all. His stock is sold. Nought remains but the house in Stillman Street."

"And his daughter?" asked Matthew, slowly.

"Aye, Susannah. She sits alone in Stillman Street. Young Ferrers that was to have wed her, and a fortune, went off to the wars to see what fortune he could win with his blade."

"Then they did not wed?"

"That they did not."

The conversation died and the English sailors made ready to go back on board ship. They bid a warm farewell to Ba-umba and his men and pledged to meet "when the plate ship shall be ready for our pleasure".

As they went to their boats, Drake turned to Matthew.

"Well, Morten, lad. Didst not expect to hear Devon voices again?"

Matthew shook his head, his heart full of what he had heard.

Drake eyed him shrewdly then said, as he stepped into the boat:

"When this business here be finished, thou'rt welcome to take passage home to Plymouth with us, lad. Hast but to ask."

Matthew stood silent watching the boats draw away. Then he turned and met Ba-umba's eyes gazing curiously at him.

Chapter twenty-five

While Drake's fleet sailed eastwards to harry Spanish shipping, Ba-umba's warriors made ready for the expedition to Panama. Matthew sailed twice round the coast to "Fort Diego" to talk to Drake's men who had been left behind to man the stronghold. They greeted him in a familiar, friendly way, as "'Maroon Boy" or "'Maroon" and were ready to talk of Plymouth. But they could tell him little more. When he asked for news of his father, they would say, "When we last saw him in church he was hale and hearty." He questioned them about Stillman Street and about Susannah. "She is as fair as ever and as proud. The maids say she doth sit in the Broad Chamber window of an evening and look out on the harbour. Else is she not to be seen."

From Drake's men Matthew learned that he was out in his reckoning. The date was December 1572. His twenty-first birthday was come and gone and he had not known. Amused, he told Ba-umba, who looked at him strangely.

"Come of age? Our boys become men long before such an age. By such an age a man may die in battle or father children. Thou art a man, though thou hast done neither." He hesitated, then said: "When we march against the Spaniards in the spring, thou wilt take thy share of gold, as do Drake's men, I think."

He laughed and clapped Matthew's shoulder.

"Look not so vexed. We have seen how thou hast changed in manner since the ships came. Speak truth. Thou wilt leave us? No?"

Matthew did not answer but walked away, angry with Ba-umba for seeing into his mind, angry at himself for not knowing what he should do. Since that night on board ship when he had flung the book given him by Susannah into the sea, his life in Plymouth had faded from his mind. Even the faces of his family had become blurred.

And now it had all been turned painfully up to the light. In his mind, as he walked about the town, or sailed along the coast, or drilled with the young warriors, would come again and again the image of a young woman seated by a window looking out over Sutton Harbour as the sun went down.

Towards the end of February, Drake and his men came back from raiding to Fort Diego. Matthew sailed round to meet them.

"Hey, 'Maroon," they greeted him. But they were in bad shape. Their faces were thin and some had the yellow cast of fever in their cheeks. Their clothes were threadbare and sea-stained. In all they had lost twenty-eight men, some in action but most from the fever. Joseph Drake had died in his brother's arms at a place they called Slaughter Island – so many men had been buried there. John Drake and a young seaman called Richard Allen had been killed boarding an enemy frigate.

"But, with such losses, are thy men in stand to march against Panama?"

Drake's beard jutted. "We'll not turn back now. We can put eighteen men in the field."

"We shall send two score of our best warriors," said Matthew.

Drake's eyes gleamed. "With that we may sack Panama itself."

"No need for that," replied Matthew. "The treasure ships are in port, and the mule train goes overland by way of Venta Cruz towards Nombre de Dios in ten days' time. Fourteen mules, eight loaded with gold, five with silver and one with jewels."

"And wilt thou march with us, Morten, lad?"

"Else wilt thou find it hard to talk with my companions."

"Thou'lt earn a double share of what we capture."

Matthew shook his head. "Nay, I'll take what thy crew take and no more."

Drake nodded. "As thou wilt. But let us delay no longer."

"Will thy men not rest?"

"Only in their graves when they hear this news."

The raiding-party set out. Drake's boats carried the sailors and warriors upstream, well into the forest. When the going became difficult, the column landed and marched into the hills. Here the trees were wide-spaced and tall, the air cool even in midday, and the going was easy.

When they came to a ridge-top, Pedro the young Cimaroon leader, who marched with Drake and Matthew, turned to the captain and said:

"Wilt thou see two great oceans at one time?"

"What's thy meaning?" asked Drake in sudden excitement.

"Why," said Pedro. "To the east lies the ocean whereon thy ships sail and to the west lies the ocean whereon sail the ships which have brought gold from the mines of Peru. At the top of this hill is a tall tree. By climbing it a man may see both oceans at the one time."

"By heaven," breathed Drake, "let's away there now."

Elated, he ran with his men to the top of the hill and clambered into the branches of the tree marked out by Pedro. From above, he shouted:

"I see it, as thou didst say, Pedro. Would God I might sail in that other sea."

"If thou might break thy ship in small pieces and carry them over the land-neck, then might thou do it," grinned Matthew as Drake reached ground again. But Drake was in no mood for jests.

164

"Nay, lad. I'll sail round to the south. If I can get ships and crews for the task."

"And who'll pay for that?" demanded Matthew.

"Why, the Spaniards," grinned Drake. And the march began again, this time downhill, away from the forests and into prairie country, where the grass, sun-dried, grew so high that they could move in it without being seen. The heat grew and the party marched on in silence through the afternoon.

As night fell, the Cimaroons and Drake's men laid their ambush in the woods above Panama. Below them gleamed the lights of the port, which was quiet, with no sign that the Spaniards suspected any danger. Matthew and a small group of Talusi, together with three men from Drake's crew crouched in the bush near the train. As soon as they heard the mule train approach, they would signal with the call of a night-bird. Then they would allow the mules to pass by and cut off the train's retreat, while Drake's party attacked from the front.

An hour passed slowly and Matthew could sense that the seamen lying near him in the undergrowth were becoming restless. "Lie still, in heaven's name," he whispered. The man next him turned and cursed. His breath reeked. He had been filling himself with spirits to keep up his courage. Matthew signalled to a warrior close by, pointing to the seaman. The warrior nodded silently.

In the distance, faint against the wind, came the sound of bells. It grew closer, more distinct.

"Lads! 'Tis here. 'Tis here!"

With a yell, the seaman sprang up, white shirt gleaming in the forest dark. The warrior seized him and dragged him down, clapping a rough hand over his mouth. But below them the sound of mule bells stopped.

Then it began again. Had the Spaniards been alerted?

Shadows loomed on the trail and the soft sound of hooves came closer. Six animals with their drivers passed by and went up the trail. But no more. From behind came a sudden commotion. Drake and Oxenham, his lieutenant, suddenly appeared on the path.

"We have been cheated. Those mules had nought but food on their backs."

"Aye," said Matthew, "thy man was drunk and gave us away."

Drake looked grim. "What's to do, then?"

"Let Pedro speak," said Matthew, "he knows the lie of the land."

Pedro spoke swiftly. "We can do two things. Go back silently, lest the Spaniard attack us, or march forward boldly and attack the rest of the train."

"Let's forward then," cried Drake, seizing Pedro by the hand.

And forward they went. With a shrill whistle from Drake and a cry of "Yo Peho" from Pedro, the raiding-party charged down the hill.

The Spaniards were waiting, a force of a score of soldiers, with pike and arquebus. As soon as they heard the shouts they opened fire blindly. Matthew, cutlass in hand, saw one of his Talusi comrades go down, shot through the head. Then they were among the Spaniards, breaking their pike rank and thrusting and cutting. At the last moment a Spanish arquebusier shot point blank as Matthew leapt on him. An explosion of light and pain threw him over on his back and he lost consciousness.

When Matthew came out of the fever that followed his wounding, he saw that he lay in Ba-umba's hut. His comrades must have carried him back through the forest and down the river. Faces moved above him, came and went — Akanoro's, Ba-umba's, and now and then the wide smile and white teeth of Kulokela's dark face. She brought him water, for his thirst was terrible, and changed the dressing on his head and face.

"Thou'rt not so handsome now," said Ba-umba, squatting by his bed. "But art not dead, as the Spaniards did intend."

Matthew's hand struggled up to the long scar that curved from forehead to cheek. It seemed completely healed.

"How long have I lain like this?"

Ba-umba shrugged.

"Ten days and more."

"What of the raid on the treasure train?"

"Our men are pleased, Drake's men are angry. We took many arms from the Spaniards, but not gold and little silver. Art sorry, Matt-ew?"

Matthew said nothing.

"Drake has now joined with a French privateer and gone to lie in wait for the silver train, but this time near Nombre de Dios. He is mad to have treasure."

Matthew tried to rise, but Ba-umba pushed him down.

"Nay, the treasure hunt is not for thee."

It was past Easter before Matthew was able to walk again and was greeted by crowds in the town, who had feared that he might die. But their boisterous pleasure in his health only made Matthew feel more sullen and guilty. He kept to himself and roamed the woods. Except where politeness demanded, he kept away from the house of Akanoro. Soon he began to go down to the shore each day in the hope of seeing Drake's ships.

Ba-umba mocked him gently.

"If thou hast not gold, thou canst not go home to England. They will have only rich men there. So must thou stay with us."

Matthew turned away angrily.

In April Drake's ships sailed into the bay. The French privateer and he had parted company on good terms. Of Drake's fleet only *The Pascha* remained, but he brought with him captured Spanish ships stocked with food and booty.

Drake's men landed to be met by the whole town. They looked like scarecrows, lean, scarred, some in rags, but one and all cheerful. Drake was jauntier than ever. He glanced at Matthew's scarred face.

"How goes it, Morten? I'm glad to see thee well, though somewhat ornamented. But I feared not to see thee again."

"How went the expedition?" said Matthew.

"In the end, all went well. We seized half a ton of silver, but the Spanish counter-attacked and we were forced to bury most of it. But what we carried away was enough to please. Forty thousand pounds we did share with the Frenchman."

He saw Matthew's face.

"'Twas pity thou could not be with us. But the crew do agree with me, that thou shalt have thy share, notwithstanding."

Matthew thanked him.

"And thou shalt have passage with us to Plymouth if that's thy wish – though thy friends here will miss thee sorely. But there is room. God knows we have enough hands and thou art more than welcome."

He turned now to salute Akanoro and Ba-umba who had come down to the shore.

"Matthew, lad. Do tell our noble friends that we will take our leave of them. Tell them that we are in their debt more deeply than we can repay, but beg of them to look over our stores and treasure. Whatsoever they will have, is theirs."

Matthew turned to Ba-umba.

"Ask Captain Drake," said Ba-umba, "if he will take with him the pinnaces he brought."

"Nay," said Drake, "they are old and battered and no more seaworthy. Why?"

"We will have the iron-work from them for spear heads and tools."

"Right willingly," said Drake. "But is there nought more precious than that?"

Ba-umba whispered awhile with Matthew. "Captain Drake. Ba-umba hath a fancy for thy sword, which thou didst have from the French privateer."

Drake smiled. "Right willingly!" Without a moment's pause he unbuckled the blade and handed it to Ba-umba, who held the carved steel aloft while the people round him murmured in admiration.

"Now, Morten, lad," said Drake. "If thou wilt come with us, then be on board in two hours' time. For my men will away. 'Tis a full year since they saw their families."

Matthew returned to his hut and sat alone for an hour, deep in thought. His thoughts pulled him both ways, to his old home and to the new. But deep down, beneath thought, was something stronger, a wish to finish uncompleted business.

He rose and began to gather together his belongings. He buckled a cutlass to his belt. But other weapons he had captured he took and distributed among the warriors who had fought with him. Then he went to Akanoro's house where the family waited for him.

"We knew that thou must go, Matt-ew," said Akanoro in his feeble, old man's voice. "If I could return to my father's home, then I would do so. But I may not, and I must make my new home where I may. May the Great Spirit watch over you as he watches over us."

Kulokela said nothing, but smiled briefly and looked down.

Ba-umba went back with him to the shore, where a canoe took them to the side of *The Pascha* in the middle of the bay.

At the last moment, as Matthew prepared to climb the side of the ship, Ba-umba held out to him a heavy canvas bag.

"Not all the gold was buried beneath the river, Matt-ew. You shall not go home a poor man. They shall not say the

Talusi are a poor and ungenerous people. If this will help you, take it."

He embraced Matthew.

"May you find your true home."

Chapter twenty-six

Drake set course north-north-east for Cape San Antonio and at first all went well. Then as they sailed by the Cape the wind shifted and drove them westward into the Gulf of Mexico.

The mate saw Drake's grim face and told Matthew: " 'Twas thus Francis and John Hawkins were driven in '68, when they took refuge in San Juan de Ulua, and were nearly trapped by the Spanish Fleet."

But after some days, Drake managed to bring the ship back to the Cape and sailed east-north-east for the Straits of Florida. They dropped anchor off one deserted shore and took turtles and eggs for the voyage. Then, meat supply secured, they set sail again. Water was short and Drake debated whether he should sail north-east to Newfoundland in the hope of meeting the Devon fishing fleet and getting fresh water, or set course for the east and try for home in the hope that water supplies would last. The crew were ready to risk the latter course – anything to get home speedily. But in the end the skies solved the problem by growing black and sending down a torrent of rain that poured into the outstretched sail and filled the barrels.

Now with the westerlies blowing strongly and making thirty leagues a day, the voyage went well. The crew made room for Matthew in the forecastle, though there was room enough, for of the seventy-three men who sailed in *The Pascha* and *Swan* in May 1572, over half had died. It was a rich voyage and each man was going home with more money than he could earn in seven years. Drake would be rich enough to match his cousin Hawkins. And Matthew – none knew what he had, though some knew he had received great wealth from his friends. But they respected him and even those who had believed the stories spread about him in Plymouth, over the loss of the slave cargo from Combe's ship, admitted he was a handy man on all counts, with a rope, a blade, a prayer or a song. They, who now thought only of the future, forgot the past. Even his name was often forgotten and the crew called him " 'Maroon Boy". In the evenings they would call, "Give us a song, 'Maroon, give us a song."

They had twenty-three days of fair winds, and at first light on the twenty-fourth the lookout in the foretop sighted Lizard Point.

"We'll be in Sutton Harbour 'afore parson's finished his sermon," shouted one of the crew.

"Nay, not so fast, lad," called his mate, "or skipper'll have us in church to hear the rest on't."

The forecast proved right and *The Pascha* sailed up Plymouth Sound just after the bells had finished their morning peal. But sharp eyes on the cliffs had spotted her, and as the Barbican at the neck of Sutton Pool came in sight, the crew from the ratlines could see an excited crowd of men, women and children pouring from the church and down St Andrew's Street and Notte Street to the quay.

"He did never finish that sermon, for there he be running with all the rest," called one of the crew. Then the men were crowding the side of the ship as she worked her way in to the jetty, shouting to the people already thronging there.

Matthew hung back away from the side and listened to the questions and answers between wharf and deck, the anxious inquiries about men who had not returned, the wild guesses at the size of the cargo, the boasts of the crew, the delighted cries of those who recognised father, husband or son.

"Why dost hide thyself, Matthew, lad?" asked Drake.

"There's none to expect me. I'll wait till all be gone and make my way home myself."

"Why so?"

"I wish that no man may know of my coming."

Drake looked at the dark scarred face, with its brown beard.

"If there is any man in Plymouth that can say the 'Maroon Boy is Jacob Morten's lost son, may I lose my fortune," he smiled.

Matthew did not answer, but formally thanked Drake for his passage home.

"Nay," Drake shook his head, "hast worked thy passage. See, Matthew, I know not if thy homecoming will bring thee joy. 'Twill not be easy. But if thou needst help, look for me by the New Quay and I'll be at thy service."

Matthew thanked him again and bade farewell. He returned to the forecastle and sat down to wait while the ship was made fast and the crew went ashore to be greeted by families and friends. An hour or so later he went on to the foredeck and looked out on the town. Sections of the wall had been repaired and strengthened, new warehouses built and cranes added to the wharf. There was the spot on the quay where John Galton and he had stood, cutlass in hand, in Satan's defence. Nay, Satan was dead, drowned in mid-ocean, and Ba-umba lived in his stead with the Talusi in their new home. He could see the church tower, and that new roof must be the Guildhall rebuilt. But there were new roofs everywhere. He could see the end of Stillman Street, but new houses obstructed his view of the Combe house. All, it seemed, had changed, grown bigger, wealthier. As he had changed. Was there a place for him?

He grew hungry and went back into the forecastle where he chewed on an old lump of bread and cheese. He'd fared better than this, he thought grimly, and no doubt he'd fare worse. On deck the shadows thrown by the mast lengthened as the day drew to its close. He must not wait too long.

He stirred himself and gathered up his gear. There was little enough of it – jacket, cutlass, and the canvas bag Ba-umba had given him. It weighed more heavily now, it seemed. He pressed it with his fingers, feeling the edges of the metal bars, twelve of them, gold and silver, a small fortune, more money than his family had ever heard of. And here was he, sneaking into Plymouth in the dusk for fear he was recognised. Why?

He avoided the Hoe Gate and skirted the walls until he came to the Frankfort Gate. Here he had raced with Charles Ferrers. Here Ferrers had cheated him. Here Ferrers had added insult to injury by beating him with a quarter staff. The insult had been avenged, he thought grimly, for he had cheated Ferrers of his wealth. But the injury?

Inside the walls, things had changed here too. On the waste ground, where his father's cottage and that of Old Tom had stood alone, new streets had been built above the church. For a while he stood baffled by the changes. Where was his home? He walked across the open ground to the first street. A small boy trotted past, heading for home. Matthew hailed him. The boy looked scared and would not stop.

"Which is Morten's cottage?"

"In front of thy nose," called back the boy over his shoulder and vanished in the dusk.

But where was the outhouse, where the yard? Where was the shippen? Matthew stared at the handsome house with its two bay windows and whitewashed walls, its new shingled roof. Now as he peered at it and slowly moved closer, he could see the lines of the old cottage. It was as though someone had taken it to pieces and rebuilt it, leaving only the general shape. But this was now no smallholder's house.

It was that of a merchant, in a small way of business, perhaps, but prosperous for all that.

As he came closer to the door, set between the two bays, he heard singing, an old hymn tune, and for a moment a wild hope rose in his heart. But the voice was not his mother's. It was a deeper, younger voice. Did Jacob Morten's new-found wealth now include servants? He stood on the doorstep. The door was open and he looked into the kitchen where the fire burned bright. It was mid-August, but his father had always loved the warmth and loved it more when he came back from prison. A dark oak table was decorated with a fine white cloth and plates were set for six people. There must be guests for supper. His glance went to the ceiling. Did his eyes deceive him, or was it lower? Yes, indeed, a new, false ceiling had been built in. Now his eyes went to the floor. Something was wrong. Where was the couch? Where was his father's couch which always stood by the wall so that the old man could look towards the church? Where was his father?

The singing came close. A woman, young, buxom and dark-haired, came into the kitchen with a bowl in her hands. "And his mercy endur . . ." She saw Matthew and screamed. The bowl dropped and shattered.

"Heaven have mercy on us. Who be you?"

Matthew stared. "I am . . ."

"Jacob. Do come quickly. There be a strange sailor in the kitchen."

Heavy footsteps sounded from above and a tramping on the stairs. His father, broad-shouldered, features red and thickened, hair now white, beard matching the snowy elegance of his collar, stepped into the room.

"Now, fellow. What is it? Is it charity you need? Then I'll bid you come back tomorrow, for I have guests here soon."

He stopped and stared. "Have I seen thy face, before?"

"Father," cried Matthew.

Jacob Morten lurched to the table and gripped the back of a chair. The woman who had knelt down to mop up the contents of the broken bowl shrieked again and ran from the kitchen.

"Is this some jest? I have but one child and he sleeps in his cradle above this room."

"I am Matthew, thy son."

"Matthew is dead in New Spain, these four, five years back. Do not mock."

Matthew came closer, into the circle of light cast by the lamp that hung over the table.

"Look on me, Father. I am thy son. Take my hand. I am alive. I did not die and they that told thee so, spoke falsely."

"Nay, it cannot be."

Matthew took the chair on his side of the table and sat down. His bundle dropped to the floor.

"Why, thou art utterly changed, Matthew. I would not have known thee."

"And thou, Father, art utterly changed. Thy legs."

His father smiled complacently.

"The Lord has restored me, in every manner."

Jacob Morten looked past Matthew, out through the door as though he waited for someone.

"That woman, Father, is she . . . ?"

"She is my wife, these twelve months since."

"And a child, too?"

"Aye, these three months since." Jacob Morten looked out again into the darkness beyond the doorway.

"Hast forgotten Mother so soon?" burst out Matthew bitterly. His father turned and stared at him. Then he rose suddenly and towered over Matthew.

"Hast not lost thy habit of passing judgment on thy father? Older art thou, but not wiser."

"But . . ."

"Speak not to me of forgetting thy mother. Where wert thou when thy mother died? Thou who might have come home with some fortune from thy voyage, cast thine own fortune away and with it the fortune of others. A double waste and all for thy vanity."

"Thou hast heard but one part of the tale," said Matthew furiously. "Wouldst thou have profit from the enslavement of others? Thou who wast deprived of thy liberty five long years?"

"Speak not to me of liberty. Thou hast taken too much liberty to thyself. Had no thought for Abraham Combe, that did give thee a place in business and home. Had no thought for Sir Henry Ferrers, a kind patron. Had no thought for shipmates, men with wives and little ones, who waited for a share of that cargo, which thou did wantonly let go. Vanity, pride was ever thy fault, Matthew Morten, and grievously have others suffered for it."

Jacob Morten sat back in his chair and looked again through the open doorway.

"Who are thy guests that do cause thee such concern?" asked Matthew.

"My wife is a niece to Mistress Combe, who now doth live with her brother in Plympton. 'Tis they and others, old friends of Abraham who sup with me tonight."

"And thou wilt not that I should sit in thy kitchen, when they come?" jeered Matthew.

His father raised his head slowly.

"I would that thou wert not in Plymouth. I would that since thou hast been the ruin of these good people, I would that thou hadst never come home, but had stayed with the savages whose good fortune thou cared more for than that of thine own kind."

In a rage Matthew stood up, his hand leaping to his cutlass.

His father smiled grimly. "God has sent thee to punish me, Matthew Morten. For thus would I have moved, when I was young and my ways were wilful and evil, even as thine."

Matthew regained his calm. "I know not why God should punish thee, but he has surely taken something from thee."

"That I am glad to lose. And if thou art glad to have it, then this home is no place for thee."

Matthew bent to pick up his bag. Akanoro's old, feeble voice, from far away, spoke in his mind. "If I could go to my father's home, I would do so. But I may not and I must make my home where I may." He strode to the door.

"Wait, Matthew. If thou hast need of money . . ."

"Nay, that is the least thing I need."

Matthew flung out through the door and brushed past a small group of people who approached. He heard their agitated voices and his father saying calmly, "Nay, 'twas but a sailor seeking charity."

"And would thou not relieve him, Jacob?"

"Nay, it was not in my power."

Chapter twenty-seven

Matthew did not slacken his pace until he reached the church. In its shadow he paused to get his breath back. Then he raced across St Andrew's Street into Whymple Street and thence into Looe Street heading down to the harbour. So Mistress Combe was supping with Jacob Morten, and Matthew Morten must not be seen? Matthew Morten was the evil doer who had robbed her husband of his fortune and beggared half the folk in Plymouth. That was the way of it? Why, he carried enough in the bag over his shoulder to make the Combe family fortune again, if he chose. The thought made him smile grimly and he slackened pace to turn into Vauxhall Street. Near the wharves the word of respectable people did not count, and the taverns as he passed sent out their light, their noise and their drunken singing. Men from Drake's ship, home with silver in their pockets, would be standing treat to the town tonight, or to the lower end of the town. The better sort were taking supper with Jacob Morten who could earn silver by reciting the word of God over sailors who risked their necks on the Spanish Main. Matthew Morten was not to be seen or heard by them. Better he vanished. Better if Plymouth, God-fearing Plymouth, still believed he was dead, and his bones lying in an island marsh in New Spain. Well, they would see.

He stopped in Stillman Street. Here was the house. Old

and ramshackle it looked now, and with but one light show-
ing. That would be the Broad Chamber. He crossed the
road and looked up. Yes, the Broad Chamber window was
open and a faint light threw shadows on the small glass
panes. Someone was above. He recrossed the street and
hammered on the door. No one came. He knocked again.
A sleepy servant girl opened the door a tiny space and asked
what he wanted. He pushed past her and leapt up the stairs,
one flight, then another. And stood at the Broad Chamber
door.

He raised a hand to knock, then dropped it again. He
pushed the door wide and entered.

Susannah sat in a chair by the window, a book in her
hand faintly lit by the candle which stood on the table. She
raised her head as he walked in, her eyes wide.

"What do you want?" Her voice expressed surprise, but
not fear.

"Susannah."

"That voice I know." She stood and raised the candle.
"The face I know not. In God's name . . ." The candle
dropped and went out. "Matthew Morten . . ."

Matthew strode two paces forward and grasped her hands.
She drew her hands back slowly but firmly and bent to
retrieve the candle. Slowly she lit it once more and stretched
out a finger to touch his scarred face.

"I am alive. 'Tis no spirit," said Matthew.

She nodded. "Art real enough, though strangely changed."

"How changed?"

"When I did know thee, thou wert good, obedient and
kind . . ."

"And now?"

"Now thou art wilful and violent. Men do as thou bid
them. Is it not so?"

"I have changed in much, Susannah, but in one thing I
am constant."

"In what?"

"In my love for thee."

She smiled. "I did think it might be so. But thou said never a word . . ."

"How could I speak? Thy father's . . ."

"My father's apprentice? Well didst thou deserve to serve that knew thy place so well."

"But now I am changed. Thou said it."

"Too late."

"Too late?"

"I am to marry Sir Charles Ferrers. That's known to thee, sir," she said lightly.

"Charles Ferrers does not want Susannah Combe. He wants her fortune."

"And that fortune is no more. Because the faithful 'prentice boy did open the door and let it go."

"Susannah. Could I but live those years again, I'd set those slaves free once more."

"So I do believe, for two good reasons."

"What good reasons?"

"One that thou art too good to grow rich from slavery. Two that thou would deny to others what thou dared not seek for thyself."

"Deny to others . . . ?"

"Aye, Matthew Morten. Did thou free those slaves only to do them good, or to do Charles Ferrers harm? I know not if love or hate be strongest in thee."

"Can I not hate Charles Ferrers, and love thee?"

"And live divided?"

Matthew turned from her and walked to the window.

"I did not mean to do thy father harm."

"But only Charles Ferrers?"

"Nay, Charles Ferrers be damned."

"Hast learnt to curse, O man of God?"

Matthew turned back.

"John Galton did once say that to me. Poor John, I did kill him with my good deed."

"Aye, Matthew Morten, hast done great harm with thy good."

"Susannah. I have brought wealth home with me, enough to repair thy family's fortune. Years have been lost but not too many to make good. If I had asked thee when I was thy father's boy to marry me, what would thou have said?"

"Aye."

"Then say it now."

"Too late."

"Why so?"

"I am promised to Charles Ferrers."

"By thy father to his father."

"I did agree."

"But so young?"

"I can stand by my word."

"But, will Charles Ferrers stand by his? Why did he not marry thee without a dowry? Why did he wait?"

She hesitated.

"Why?" demanded Matthew.

"Charles Ferrers is proud."

"Proud, insolent and overbearing."

"He has walked in the shadow of his father all his life. He has sought to find his own name."

"Slaying for gold?"

"As others slay for God."

"He left thee."

"Before he did, he freed me from my bond and said he would come and ask again. He shall be free to do so."

"As I am free to ask thee now, Susannah. Charles Ferrers is far away."

She looked at him gently.

"How strange thou art, Matthew Morten. When thou speakest for others, how generous. When thou speakest on thine own behalf, how mean."

"In this I will be selfish."

She nodded. "Charles Ferrers is in Plymouth."

"He has come back and not sought thee out?"

"I wait him by the hour."

"Then tell him no."

"I must first hear what he has to say."

He walked towards the door.

"I'll go away now, but I'll come back and ask thee once more."

"As you wish."

He opened the door to go, but Susannah stopped him.

"Hast thou the book I gave thee still?"

"Nay. I cast it into the sea."

He ran down the stairs and out into the street. As he did so, a man waiting in the shadows ran off before him and turned aside into Vauxhall Street.

Matthew strode on towards the quay, but as he went seemed to hear footsteps behind him.

Chapter twenty-eight

Matthew turned into a tavern hard by the Dung Quay, where he had drunk five years before with John Galton. It was little changed. The landlord was the same. He paid no heed to Matthew as he sat down near the door, but served him with spiced wine. Nor did the men around pay him much attention. Over in the far corner sat a group of men from Drake's ship, but they were too far gone in their drink to pay heed to Matthew.

He drank slowly and in silence, then ordered more wine, bread and meat. He was suddenly aware that he had eaten little but bread and cheese since dawn. An old sailor sat down by him.

"What hast thou in that bag that thou dost grip so fiercely? Hast come home with a treasure?"

"Nay, 'tis not worth so much."

"Is't enough to buy an old sailor a drink?"

Matthew laughed.

"Why, yes. Here."

The old man took the coin. "Do I know thy face?"

"I doubt it." But the old man went on staring at him.

"There is that in thy face that puts me in mind of the young boy that did sing so sweetly in church these many years past. What was his name?"

"Nay, old man, go drink thy ale. Thou'rt light-headed."

"My eyes be old, but I do never forget a face I have known. Wait but one moment and I'll have it."

"Nay, off with thee," Matthew spoke irritably.

"Morten, Matthew Morten, that be it. Thy face be changed, and scarred and blackened by the sun, but if y'be not Matthew Morten then I'm a Turk."

Men at the next table turned and listened. One of them stood.

"What didst say, old man?"

"He said nought for thine ears," replied Matthew.

"He did say Morten," insisted the sailor and came close to the table. In that instant Matthew recognised him. It was a deckhand from *The Golden Way*, a young lad they called Dickon. In that same moment, Dickon recognised him.

"Why, 'tis that devil Morten!" he exploded. "Lads," he called to the other table. "Look what an ill wind hath blown to our shores. Him we did think was dead."

The other men rose. There were four of them and two of them were unsteady on their feet, but the other two looked sober and all faces were hostile. They were men from *The Golden Way*, all of them, and they stood now in a half-circle between his table and the door. Matthew pushed his stool gently back until he felt his back touch the wall.

"Aye, that be Matthew Morten, that did loose our cargo and beggar us all," said one. "We thought he were dead, but God, or the Devil, hath sent him back to our shores."

Matthew looked to the right. Drake's men, busy with their drinking, were paying little heed to his corner, thinking, no doubt, it was just another bunch of old shipmates meeting. Not that in their state he could count on much help from them.

"Now," said Dickon. "I know what we'll do. We'll go fetch Harry Churler, that's what we'll do. He'll know how we should deal with Morten."

"No need for that," came a cheery call from the tavern door. All turned, and Matthew took his chance to push back his chair and stand up against the wall. At the inn door, his face aglow with satisfaction, his red hair and beard seemingly untouched, he looked as amiable, as evilly cheerful as he had ever done. But who was that beside him? That young man in green velvet and magnificent ruff, with his curled moustache and insolent smile? Charles Ferrers.

Suddenly Matthew felt his mind at rest. He laughed out loud.

"Why, what companions in mischief have we here? What does Sir Charles Ferrers with a murdering hound like Harry Churler?"

Churler's mouth drooped.

"Aye, Harry. Do thy shipmates know that thou tried to murder me that day, and only by the grace of God did I escape? Thou didst shoot me in the back, cowardly dog that thou art."

Matthew's sudden attack took the seamen by surprise, but Ferrers viewed him coolly.

"I have no concern with thy private quarrels, Morten. I am hear to call thee to account on a public matter."

"What public matter?"

"That by thy action thou didst bring ruin on the families of some three and twenty men of this town, men of great and small estate."

"Aye," jeered Matthew, "thy plans were wrecked on that shore, were they not, Ferrers? Thou sought to marry Susannah Combe for her estate and when the estate vanished, so did thine ardour cool."

The blood spread in Ferrers's face, but he kept calm.

"Thou and I have a private quarrel, 'tis true, Morten, since the day I thrashed thee."

"And cheated me."

"Talk not of cheating. Thou hast cheated these men and others not now alive out of their fortune."

"If there be any sailor in Plymouth," said Matthew, "who suffered loss of his wages for that voyage, I will make them good. But I will not make good shares in a cargo such as *The Golden Way* did carry. Nor, Charles Ferrers, will I provide a dowry so that thou canst sue for Susannah Combe's hand at thy pleasure."

"By God, Morten, that last is too much. Defend thyself."

At Charles Ferrers's shout, and the clash as his blade met Matthew's, Drake's men in the corner stopped their drinking and looked up wild-eyed. One staggered to his feet and started for the door. Men at tables round drew back, caught up stools and cleared a circle. The blades clashed, clashed again, hilts strained together, then the two flew apart.

"Hast learned thy lessons, Morten," jeered Ferrers.

"And battle with men has made thee drop thy tricks, Ferrers," replied Matthew, and, lunging forward, he made the cutlass steel whir like a bird's wing as he drove Charles headlong across the tavern floor. A quick slash laced Ferrers's knuckles with blood and the sword flew from his grasp. A sailor snatched it up. Matthew gestured wth the point of his blade and the man threw the weapon back to Ferrers.

Ferrers held his right hand to his mouth a second to staunch the bleeding, then without warning hurled himself forward and it was Matthew's turn to retreat before the murderously stabbing sword.

"Look out astern, 'Maroon," sang out one of Drake's men.

Too late, Matthew felt both his elbows seized from behind and Harry Churler's hot breath on his neck. Ferrers gaped as he saw Matthew helpless, but his headlong rush carried him on and he drove the sword point in at Matthew's heart.

As the point pierced clothing and skin, Matthew's body, as if by its own will, gave a great shuddering flinch to the side. The blade drove on, scoring his ribs. Behind him Churler gave a whimpering shriek. His grip on Matthew's elbows relaxed and his weight slithered down Matthew's back to collapse on the floor. Matthew sprang to one side, cutlass at the ready. Churler's body lay sprawled against the wall, his mates standing by horrified and helpless. But none could match the expression of horror on Ferrers's face as he saw Churler's body and gazed on his own bloodstained blade.

"Hast had enough?" called Matthew. "Or wilt thou dispatch more of thy clients?"

Desperately Ferrers guarded himself, but Matthew, heedless of the pain from his ribs, was on him. With hacking, slashing strokes he bore Ferrers across the floor. With one sweep he smashed the blade from his hand and then, with a red haze of hate before his eyes, he swung his cutlass back above his left shoulder to cut down on Ferrers's neck.

"Matthew!"

Someone screamed his name. The blade halted in mid-air. His eyes cleared and he saw Ferrers's face contorted with fear, hands raised to protect his neck. He dropped the cutlass point and turned to the tavern door. Susannah stood there, and with her Francis Drake and several of his crew.

"Put up thy blade, Morten, lad," called Drake, and Matthew pushed his cutlass back into his belt. "Mistress Combe has saved thee from a great crime. Enough death here tonight." He gestured to Churler's body, which the landlord and two sailors were now dragging from the room.

"I did warn thee there were men in Plymouth that would have revenge on thee."

"We did not intend to take Morten's life," said Dickon. "We did but seek right for our wrong and Sir Charles did take our part."

"Aye," said Matthew bitterly, "and did further his own private quarrel in the same time. 'Twould have been well for thee if I had died, Ferrers."

"And for thee, if I had died," retorted Ferrers.

"Peace," cried Susannah. "What kind of creature would I be that would fly to one who had slain the other? If I did think men brawled over my name in taverns, I'd be a nun."

"Well spoken, Mistress Combe," said Drake. "Let Ferrers and Morten both pledge us here that while they live in Plymouth they will not quarrel."

Matthew and Ferrers faced one another and nodded. Matthew turned to Susannah.

"Now shalt thou give thine answer, finally. Who wilt thou wed?"

She gazed at him quietly.

"Matthew, what can I say? Our ways did part full five years past when thou didst believe only wealth could win me."

"And did it not?" cried Matthew.

"No, nor has it yet, nor will it, neither the wealth thou hast nor the wealth Charles Ferrers has not."

"But his name . . ."

"Is his name greater than thine? If thou believe so, thou art less than I thought thee."

"Then thou wilt marry Ferrers?"

"He asked me. I did say yes."

"Then," said Matthew, "it is done. I have no more business here."

He turned to Drake.

"I'll ask of thee a favour. That thou wilt take this store of mine," he raised the bag from the tavern floor and flung it on the table, "and use it to see that no man of the crew of *The Golden Way*, nor woman nor child of their kin, do now go hungry." He glanced at Susannah and Charles. "I think not on those who ventured their wealth on this voyage, as they did in the expectation of rich return. I think on those who ventured their lives."

He looked round the crowded tavern. "Well, men do hold me at fault for what I did and say it was for wilful pride or for revenge. No matter. There are men who know me otherwise. But in Plymouth have I no more life to live. Here I was a lad that did have foolish dreams and foolish dreams are no more for me. I'll take my gear and be gone."

With that Matthew Morten left the tavern and next day went from his native town for ever.

From the captain's journal, the *Prince Harry* out of Falmouth, 15th November, year of our Lord, 1573:

"Last night we lost our young boatswain, Morten of Plymouth, a good seaman and a godly man, beloved for his piety and good humour.

"He was last seen by the larboard watch when we lay off New Spain, some ten leagues from Nombre de Dios. The night was clear, the sea calm, and we lay but a bow shot from the shore.

"The crew say he did tell them more than once that there was a goodly land hereabouts where a man might be merry; they mocked him and did say none lived in these parts but Spaniards and poor savages. He did smile and swear he spoke truth, that he had seen it once and was minded to see it again.

"May heaven's mercy attend him, where'er he be."

Bess

ROBERT LEESON

Bess Morten's flight from her overbearing guardian leads her to the New World in search of her brother Matthew. Determined and spirited, Bess has to fight for her right to independence, love, and to achieve the future she believes in.

This is an excellent adventure story and a sequel to *Maroon Boy*.

Bess is a character that 'ought to place her high among the fictional heroines with readers of today'.

British Book News

The White Horse
ROBERT LEESON

In this sequel to 'Maroon Boy' and Bess, Matt, Bess's son – the proud 'blackamoor' from New England – lands in Plymouth during the Civil War. He is haunted by dreams of a white stallion which comes to symbolise his quest – to avenge the wrong done to his mother and the murder of his father by the ruthless Sir Ralph Ferrers.

Matt's courage and uncompromising search for the truth takes him into many unexpected situations in this exciting adventure novel.

Complete in itself, *The White Horse* concludes a magnificent trilogy.

Beyond the Dragon Prow

Robert Leeson

The prophecy at Stiglaf's birth, the crippled son of a Viking war lord, of never ruling his people seems to be coming true. When his father dies, he is challenged to the leadership by his cousin Torald, and forced to flee the land. His wanderings lead him into many exciting adventures with his unusual companions and Stiglaf proves to have other strengths, which enable him to fulfil the prophecy in a strange and positive way.

'A good story, exciting, fast moving, easy to read'
Children's Book Review

Tig's Crime
T. R. BURCH

The body of a midget newspaper seller in an alleyway . . . a robbery accidentally witnessed . . . two scruffy street musicians . . . a gang of children wanting a penny for the guy . . . They all connect in Tig's mind, they are all pieces in a very sinister puzzle. But fourteen-year-old Tig, a truant both from school and from his unhappy home, has trouble getting anyone to believe his story; a story that some would rather remained untold. Alone and in danger, he roams the streets in the chill November fog, always watching, always watched, in an attempt to see justice done.

Tig's Crime is a superbly written fast-moving adventure. 'Has chilly excitement on every page. But like all the best thrillers it is the final few paragraphs which hold the biggest shock of all.'

Daily Telegraph